# THE HOUSE on the EDGE

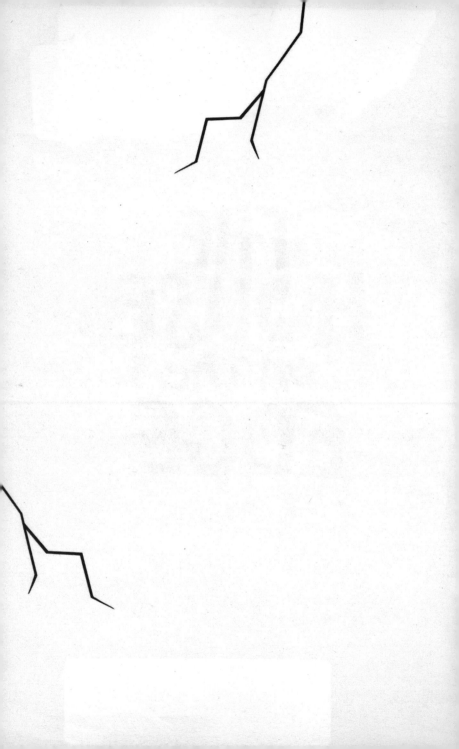

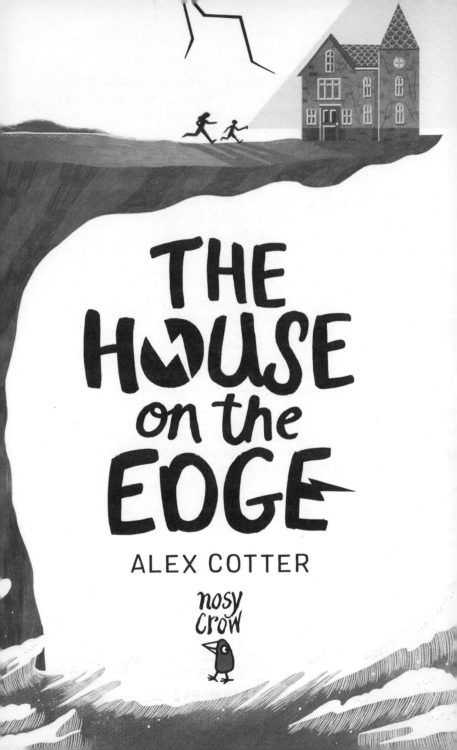

# THE HOUSE
## on the
# EOGE

ALEX COTTER

nosy crow

First published in the UK in 2021 by Nosy Crow Ltd
The Crow's Nest, 14 Baden Place
Crosby Row, London SE1 1YW

www.nosycrow.com

ISBN: 978 1 78800 862 4

A CIP catalogue record for this book is available from the

*For Mae*

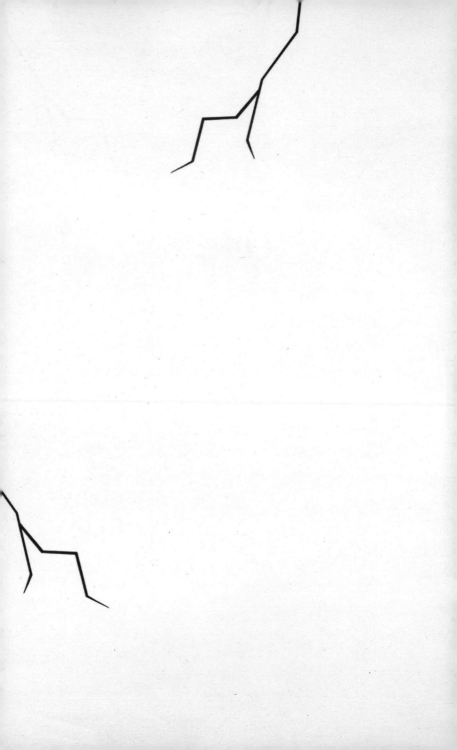

# One

Mum wasn't always this way. Though without a TARDIS, I can see why you might find that hard to believe. You just see what's in front of you. Like people walk along the beach and they'll look up and spot The Lookout. Rising tall and uneven – teetering – right at the edge of the cliff. And their very first thought is: *Blimey, that house is going to topple any minute!* I swear I see those exact words written on their faces. Sheer fear. That our pebbledash cream walls, our stained slate roof might suddenly fall. Flatten them against the sand, like Dorothy's house landing on the Wicked Witch of the East. When actually – things take much longer to fall than that, right?

"Noah! Answer me: Rice Krispies or Cheerios?"

You have to shout a question to Noah, and you have to shout it at least four times. Before he emerges from deep inside his head, like some hibernating hedgehog blinking into the light – *Someone wants me?* Away with the fairies, Dad calls it, when Noah glazes over like he's fixed to a phone. Except Noah never needs a screen.

"Huh?" He lifts his eyes finally. They look bloodshot and swollen. I heard him creep downstairs again last night.

"*Krispies* or *Cheerios*?" I shake both boxes impatiently. I don't even know why I give him the choice.

Noah mumbles, "Krispies," in a tone like it's the obvious answer. When last week all he ate was Cheerios. He starts studying me as I pour him a bowl, slop in milk.

"Did you hear it last ni—?" he asks carefully.

"*No!*" I say, before he can finish the question, rolling my eyes for extra measure.

"You really didn't hear anything?" Noah sits back, incredulous, wedging both hands in his thick red hair so it stands to attention.

"Uh huh, that's what 'no' means," I tell him, ignoring the niggle in my tummy. What I heard, I remind myself stiffly, are the noises any ancient house by the sea makes: gulls shriek, radiators tick, waves crash, beams creak.

"You can shape sounds into whatever you want," I tell him in the grown-up, sing-song voice I use a lot lately. "Like the way you can make star signs fit your life." Which makes me think briefly of Asha (when I'm really trying my best not to), checking hers every day.

"I'm not making it up." Noah pulls his sulky face. All eyebrows and bottom lip.

I shrug dismissively and turn to put the milk back. I've decided it's best not to give him a "platform". That's the posh word this pamphlet in the school library used. All right, so the pamphlet was about OCD and phobias and stuff. But I reckon it'll have the same result. If I don't encourage Noah's fantasies, if he's no one to share them with, hopefully he'll stop having them altogether.

"Aw, *Noah*, will you give off night raiding," I groan, staring into the empty fridge. "I'll have to shop again now!"

"I haven't; it's not me!" Noah complains. Before we both glance up at the familiar creaking sounds above. The house's way of saying: *she's awake at last*. I zip back to the cluttered kitchen counter: kettle for tea, bread in toaster; while I wait: load dishwasher, pack lunches.

"Eat!" I remind Noah what he's supposed to be doing as I rush out with a mug of milky tea and some heavily buttered toast. Calling back, "You don't want to be late," because it's something Mum would say. The Other Mum that is. The one you'd need a TARDIS to know about.

I slow my pace only when I've passed through our tiled, dim alleyway of a hall and I'm facing the stairs alongside our many-greats-grandfather clock. It started after Dad upped and left, I suppose, so that'll be four months and two days ago. (I can give you hours if you want.) I started worrying about our house. Like, really worrying. Just like Dad used to. He says old houses have voices. Now all I hear are The Lookout's creaks and groans whenever we move. Like every tread I take, up the wonky stairs, or across the uneven wooden floors above, gives it pain.

It's called The Lookout because our ancestor, Tom Walker, who built it, lit his lantern to warn ships about the rocks below. But I like to think it's because it takes care of us. Which is why it's imperative! Quintessential! Unequivocal! And every other big word! That I look after it back. So I climb daintily, like it's some test and if I fail monsters will get me – moving my feet to the part of the stairs I know are more solid; putting most of my weight on the scratched wooden bannister. Even though the extra strain in my arms makes me think of being little and on Dad's back on walks; trying my best to be as light as possible so he won't remember he says I'm getting too heavy to be carried.

The usual small animal noises are coming from

the bathroom up on the landing. It's where Mum does most of her crying. I think she reckons if she runs the sink we won't hear. I pause outside; a weak hand to the door. Then I carry on. Into Mum's bedroom, where it's still night-time and it smells of oversleeping and stale breath; musty, like you get in charity shops.

I make space for the tea and toast on her cluttered bedside table, and quickly reach to draw back the curtain for, *hooray, light*. Hurriedly yank open the wonky window: an impatient burst of cold air rushes in, like it's been waiting pressed up against the glass all night. The sea gets busy; salt and seaweed set to work on the stuffiness; the rush and smash of waves fill the silence. I'm watching a kestrel hovering motionless above the cliff edge and wondering how it stays so still, when there's a creak of floorboard; a sniff; a sigh. And Mum appears in the doorway.

"Faith, I keep telling you, you don't need to bring me my breakfast, love." Her voice – it's nothing like it used to be either. The sound of it makes my insides feel empty. It's too whispery and feathery, like one cough or a sneeze and it'll fly away completely.

And – *err, yes, I do*, otherwise she doesn't eat.

"Mmm, yum," she says, coming over to take a mouse bite of toast, her appreciation-smile looking as exhausted as her eyes and bones. She has on the same pair of Dad's old blue pyjamas. She rarely gets dressed these days. She's forever saying, "I'll get up soon." *Yeah, right.* She's been in bed so long that the back of her hair's a permanent nest. Her skin's starting to look as grey as the sea mist outside.

She climbs back under the covers while I tell her I need money to buy food later. I try to keep my eyes from drifting to the side where Dad used to sleep. To his bedside table, where his reading glasses are still sitting on top of his book: *Dorset Wreckers*, whoever they are.

"Noah can come home by himself," I say, adding an impatient, "Lots of Year Fives walk back alone," when she makes a groaning sound.

"They all live right in town, not at the edge of it," Mum says, fumbling for her credit card from her purse. She holds my eyes as I take it. Hers are watery. "I think I heard Noah going downstairs again in the night," she says timidly.

I look away to roll my eyes. *Hold the front page.* Noah's been going down to the cellar *every* night, for the past two weeks or so. I know that, because I'm the one who has to go out and shout, "Back to bed!" Yeah, OK, so lately, the one who pulls her covers over her head and ignores him. I hate going anywhere near the cellar, especially at night, especially after Dad told us it's not *safe* to go down there!

*Then why don't* you *do something to stop him?* Mean Me wants to tell her. Except I won't, because I'm already fearing what comes next.

"Maybe you and Noah should go and stay with your Uncle Art and Aunty Val after all."

My heart turns into a fist. I glance back at the perfectly-still kestrel and suck in a deep breath of salt and seaweed. I've got to play this right. Talking about it last week ended with me shouting and Mum sobbing uncontrollably.

"I told you, we don't need them. Noah and I've got everything covered." I swallow back a stream of acid that enters my mouth. "I'll stop Noah getting up in the night, OK? Just don't even go speaking to Uncle Art!"

Uncle Art can't know Mum's in bed all day. He can't know she's wearing the same pair of pyjamas for weeks on end. He definitely can't find out about Noah hearing weird voices in the cellar. My chest's getting tight. He can't know I'm doing all the work: cooking, washing, fixing. He'll use it as an excuse. I know he will. A coldness spreads over my body that doesn't come from the open window. Uncle Art is just waiting for a reason to get us out of here and have The Lookout condemned.

When I look back again, Mum's biting her lip hard, like I do when I want to stop myself from crying. "I can't ... can't ... can't," she starts telling the bedspread. It's something else she's forever saying. *You can't what?* Mean Me nearly snaps back, a sudden blaze of anger heating my stomach. *Can't work out the square root of pi? Can't wait to watch Strictly? Can't bear Facebook?*

"Faith?" Mum pleads, like she can hear inside my head.

I drop my chin to my chest and mumble, "Promise you won't call Uncle Art."

The waves get louder, till she finally whispers, "OK, I promise," and the coiled snake that lives in my stomach these days settles down again. I start being as busy as the sea. Showing her we can manage very well without Uncle Art and Aunty Val, thank you very much. I pick up a crusty cardy from the floor, a mug of yesterday's tea; make a tower of some paperbacks. Before I take quick, soft steps across the floorboards to the door, with a la-di-da, how-responsible-am-I, "Can't be late for school!"

"Send Noah up for a goodbye kiss," I hear Mum call out as I reach the stairs. Even shouting, her voice stays fragile and flimsy. Like she's miles away or sinking fast into quicksand. Whenever I try to remember the sound of her old voice, the way she used to belly-laugh, and sing daft songs and holler "Dinner!" – even the way she'd argue with Dad in the months before he left – I can't. Maybe you only hear what's in front of you too.

I'm back downstairs with our many-greats-grandfather clock, when I start to feel dizzy. Something's coaxing my stomach snake. I press my hand against the clock's solid shiny wood to steady myself. It was passed down with The Lookout to our great-greats over three centuries. "And what about the many-great grandmothers?" Old Mum used to say. The fact The Lookout wasn't passed to women, she said, was another reason to leave. Before Dad went, all she did was list reasons to go (*"It's too isolated!"* *"Too cold!"* *"Too unfixable!"*). I hear Dad argue back (*"It's my home!"* *"I can fix it!"*).

My stomach snake slinks upwards through my chest. I pincer my lips and fix my mind on the clock's creamy-white face instead – the pastel picture above the numerals that I've always loved. It's of an old house at sunset, leaning over the top of a cliff while a ship passes below. It never tells the time. The family story goes that ancestor Tom Walker stopped it working the day his daughter died. Removed the pendulum; threw away the key. I trace a finger where his initials T.W. and an X are carved into the wood. "Not a kiss," Dad said ages ago when I asked, "but

Tom's reminder to keep the clock door locked and sealed shut ever since."

My stomach snake hisses and attacks. *Dad* again. I pull my hand from the clock like it's burned me. I don't understand why my dad would just up and leave, without even a goodbye. If I listen to Mum, he needs time to himself; if I think like Noah, he's been taken by pirates. But I don't think like Noah.

I prefer not to wonder where Dad is. The snake retreats.

Like that OCD pamphlet said, it's better not to give some thoughts a "platform".

# Two

"Is it any bigger?" I say, as Noah joins me in the back garden, *finally* done with saying goodbye. *Mummy's boy.*

He exhales loudly and, typical Noah, doesn't answer the question but asks one of his own. "Will Mum be OK?"

"Course, stupid!" I straighten up. He's making his worried eyes. His hands are bunched in the pockets of his grey school trousers that are an inch too small for him, revealing odd socks (one red, one spotty; both holey).

"She just needs some rest still." It's

my new I-have-all-the-answers voice. Cheery. I don't even say anything when Noah takes Dad's precious brass telescope out of his coat pocket, putting it to his eye. When Noah knows he's supposed to keep it safe inside, in the lounge with the old lantern. Both are inscribed with T.W. just like on our many-greats-grandfather clock.

"I'm going to *wish* for something," Noah says, as if I've just asked what he's doing. "But there's no point telling you what it is."

"Suits me," I say, my voice a shrug. Dad used to try and convince us Tom Walker's old maritime telescope was magical. Which obviously I know now is a load of old rubbish. But Noah still likes to believe in lots of things.

"I'm wishing ... that you'd listen for once," he continues importantly, with a dramatic pause. "About the sea ghost in our cellar who I need to help. I told him that Dad—" He stops abruptly at the grunt noise from the back of my throat. We both know we never actually mention the Dad word *out loud*.

I try again: "Noah – I *said*, is it any bigger?"

There's another pause while the question journeys to the responsive part of my little brother's brain. Eventually, he pulls the telescope away and concentrates on The Crack by my feet. The three-metre gash in our back garden that we've been watching like it's a sleeping python since it appeared overnight a week ago. Noah bends closer. The sky seems to come with him, elephant grey and sombre, as if it's inspecting The Crack too.

He cocks his head to one side and says "Mmm" and "I see" like he's some expert on *Antiques Roadshow*. Which he is in a way. Noah's always been good at observing stuff, spotting things. Things that others don't. He finds all the lost items people leave on the beach, and all the new objects the waves sweep in, when the sea's having its spring clean. It's why his bedroom permanently smells like an aquarium, and looks like a museum, since Mum stopped making him tidy it.

"I think it might have grown a little at that end – and got deeper there," Noah points, scrunching his mouth up for "sorry".

I clamp my thumbnail between my teeth and stare up at The Lookout. Half a dozen small windows gaze back at me, like it's waiting for me to pass on Noah's prognosis. There are only about seven metres between The Crack and our back door. About five the other way, from The Crack to the garden fence. Which is also the edge of the cliff. If it gets any longer, any deeper, it could split our garden in two. Our house too. I rip the end of my nail off and spit it out. Right as Vicious Wind starts circling. It whips brown strands out of my ponytail, using them to thrash my eyes. I never knew I could hate the wind so much. Hissing and howling like invading warriors. Rattling the pipes on the house, playing xylophone with the slates; bringing its friend, Storm, to shave the cliff below, as easily as stripping bark from a tree.

"Give me that," I say, with a bite I don't mean, and grab the brass telescope from Noah. Without really thinking, I lift it to my eye, hard against my socket, steeling myself to hear Dad's voice. Like you hear the sea in a conch shell. *Close your eyes and make your wish. Open your eyes, and –* "Surprise!" Dad would sing – as a pile of presents *magically* appeared through its lens.

But there are no birthday fairies, like there is no magic – because The Crack in our garden is still there when I re-open my eyes. I grind my teeth, feeling stupid for making the wish in the first place, and swing the telescope around, anywhere but the house, The Crack, the cliff – to a giant tanker on the grey horizon; a fishing boat nearer shore; a couple of dog walkers on Redstone Beach; a boy in an oversized blue parka. I stay with the boy. He's crouching, like he's searching for something. He'd better not be a fossil hunter. I hate them almost as much as Vicious Wind. Chipping at the cliff face with their tiny hammers, not caring that the last landslip took away our old garden fence.

I hand the telescope back to Noah, pointing out Blue Parka. "You might have a customer." Noah gets excited about helping people find their missing things. Except – maybe not today. "Mum'll take you to school again soon, all right?" I translate his silence. Before I tug him towards the back door, Vicious Wind zipping in and out of our legs like it wants to trip us up. While, inside my head, I make another wish, probably for the zillionth time: that I wasn't the oldest.

Now we're *really* running late. Because: *no,* Noah hadn't brushed his teeth. And then: *oh, no,* he's *not* remembered to put underwear on. "Would you forget to wee if I didn't remind you?" I ask breathlessly. We're having to run-walk and that's making the worry-pains in my gut worse. They usually come as soon as I can't see the house any more. When the town starts to gradually creep up on us, after we've taken our shortcut along the cliff path above Redstone Beach; round the Second World War pillbox; across the field near the disused well; past Halfpenny Farm and the giant oak; through the metal kissing-gate into St Swithun's church. Before we rejoin the main road and its rows of brick houses with blank faces and people in coats and cars, on bikes and phones. Noah and I both jump at the thrum of the number 44 passing too close to the pavement, on its way to the bus station, then Tesco, then the big town – where Uncle Art lives. *Uncle Art.* My guts threaten to explode.

We start running for real as Noah's school bell rings in the distance, sprinting as we round the playground to his class door. I shove him inside when he comes to an abrupt standstill, even though I know just how he feels. I make one of Old Mum's cheesy thumbs-ups when he looks back uncertainly, holding it till he's lost to the cloakroom. Then I check the time on my phone – five minutes till my bell goes – and launch back into run mode.

"Noah's sister! A word, please!"

I should have known this day was only going to get worse.

Mrs Hollowbread. Noah's ancient teacher. Tight hair bun; broad shoulders; wrinkled prune-mouth sucking on a lemon. She knows my name. She just chooses never to use it. I've an urge to keep going, pretend I've not heard, but I've got to seem responsible, so – "Yes?" I say, bright-and-breathless. Out of the corner of my eye, I notice a boy around my age move down the other side of the railings. I recognise the oversized blue parka he's wearing – the boy on the beach before.

"I told you last week, I need your mother to come in and speak with me," Mrs Hollowbread says, her voice as brittle as the cuttlefish you find dried-up on the shore. "I'm concerned about Noah."

"Still?" I ask innocently. "Umm, she can't right now. A cold."

Mrs Hollowbread narrows her sharp eyes to paper slits, but I can still read them. I can read all the gossip that's spreading through the town, as fast and furious as Vicious Wind. That no one's seen Mum for months. That they'd do this or that, if it were them. That ah, the poor children. And oh, what's to be done!

"*Everyone* should make time for their children," Mrs Hollowbread eventually answers, using a tone aimed to sting. I swear I can see tentacles growing out of her body.

Parka Boy is leaning over the railing now, frown lines on his forehead, like he's straining to hear the conversation. *What's his problem?*

"I'll get her to call you," I say, already trying to work out how I'll make Mum's feathery voice be heard down the phone. How I'll force her to say the right things: *Yes sir, no sir, three bags full sir.* What if she cries? What if she starts her, *I can't, can't, can't?* What if they decide together, we should go to Uncle Art's? My heart pumps faster. I clench my hands into fists to stop them shaking. Mum can't call anyone. Not yet.

"Maybe I can help instead?" I say, employing grown-up, sing-song voice.

Which doesn't wash with Mrs Hollowbread. The lemon in her mouth turns to cyanide; she brandishes a folder from under her arm. I realise too late that she clearly planned this ambush. "I suppose you've seen these?"

I gaze down at the pictures she's showing me, recognising them as Noah's handiwork straight away. Pencil drawings of distorted faces; flowing hair and missing teeth; popping eyes that look bloodshot even without colour. He's a good artist, my brother, but I can see Mrs Hollowbread's not interested in his talent. I sniff and try to keep my expression casual, even appreciative. "He has a unique perspective," I primly repeat something I heard Mum tell his last teacher, when she was Old Mum and taking care of all things Noah.

"Other children have seen them!" The morning air's cold enough that she blows out dragon's breath with her outrage. "What's wrong with animals and flowers? What on earth makes him want to draw like this? Horrid video games?"

I make a definite shake of my head.

"Then who is filling his head with *horror*?" Mrs Hollowbread eyes me accusingly. As if I'm one of those sisters like Asha, who teases her twin brothers about nuclear war and alien invasions till they cry and tell on her. All I do is make Noah eat and wash, and wear underpants!

"He's scaring the other children! Giving Edie Miller nightmares, her father says. About sea ghosts beneath his house!"

I take a step back like someone's shoved me. My heart zips to race-car speed. "That's not true." *It's just my house's voice; the sounds of the sea!*

"Well, of course it's not true!" Mrs Hollowbread

almost shrieks. "I've made it very clear to Noah. Ghosts do not exist – sea or otherwise!"

I glance at Parka Boy. He's scratching his frowning head now.

"Are you listening to me, Noah's sister?" Mrs Hollowbread forces my eyes back to her. "Your mother must make Noah a priority! Tell her, I'll visit her at home."

"That's not possible!" I hear myself shout back before I can stop.

Mrs Hollowbread's prune-mouth turns shrivelled raisin. "Is there a problem with my seeing your mother?" she says, her words tight and stiff.

"No, I mean..." I flounder. "You don't need to ... because, because..." Which is when it dances on to my tongue, gliding out of my mouth like a swan through water, the word I *never* use out loud. "Dad will come and see you." My mouth widens into a smile, like my lips delight in the dangerous words. "If you can just wait a few weeks."

I notice Parka Boy starting to smile too. I scowl at him to butt out.

"Your father?" Mrs Hollowbread says, her sharp eyes confused.

"That's right, he called to let us know he'll be home soon." My voice gains confidence, like I'm back performing in the school plays I used to love. I even picture it – like it really happened! – the landline ringing and: "Hello, Starling!" Dad's nickname for me that I'd started to find mega-embarrassing.

"Yeah, we're all really excited!" I finish my performance, ready for a gush of *How wonderful, your father – home in time for Easter!*

Except she says none of that. Her expression remains rock hard, the shrivelled raisin disappearing into an invisible line. "*Either* parent needs to contact me, *urgently*."

I don't lie. I'm not a liar. Least not big, fat, whopper lies. But this lie feels so sweet on my tongue, I can't help telling it again, my encore if you like. "Dad will sort everything out!"

# Three

*What was I thinking?* I'm so mad with myself, I no longer care that I might miss registration. I stomp harder against the pavement. My big fat lie following me, zapping at my head like an angry bee. Down the high street, past the Co-op and the fossil shop, past the motor-mouthed parents crowding out The Teapot, making its window steam from their hot breath. No doubt talking about us. Our small town sucks up gossip like a Hoover and spits it out in every direction. I walk even faster. What if my lie reaches Mum? I see her springing out of bed at Dad's homecoming, like Grandpa Joe in *Charlie and the Chocolate Factory* – only to sink down, even lower, when she realises: I made it all up.

"Don't let her get to you!"

I jump at the strange voice at my side. Dark hair, and frown lines. Eyes as navy blue as his zipped-up parka.

"Do I *know* you?" I say, and I don't care how rude I sound.

He grins, a wide one that shows crooked front teeth and makes a left dimple. "I'm Sam." Parka Boy pushes forward a hand to shake mine like we're grown-ups. It looks grubby, so I don't. I notice his clothes look dirty too, and he smells of the sea. On his feet, he's wearing blue crocs with socks (what Sian would call "a fashion No Way"). And those black trackie bottoms, school will send him home for. I make a mental shrug: *not my problem*. I don't concern myself with Other People any more.

"That teacher." He thumbs back over his shoulder. His accent sounds sort of northern. "She giving you a hard time?" He starts swinging his arms as we walk.

"What's it got to do with you?" I mumble. Why does everyone in this town have to know my business?!

Grubby Sam lifts his chin. "She's my gran. I'm Sam Hollowbread." He says his name slowly, like he's really proud of being related to that battleaxe.

"Lucky you," I reply sarcastically.

Not that he notices; he's spitting out his next words like they're boiling hot. "But don't tell anyone! Promise? She's a bit funny about me living with her. Not ha-ha funny," he adds, and laughs, "she's not in stiches over it or anything." He keeps laughing. One of those tickly infectious laughs, like yawns can be, and I feel a bubbling beneath my ribs. Which is easy to stop. I just think about The Crack – longer and deeper in my mind.

"Good news about your dad, though." Sea-smelling Sam breaks into my nightmare.

"What *didn't* you hear?" I say bluntly, then: "Your gran didn't seem to think so." The lie is back swatting at my head again.

"Well, dads don't usually come back." He scrunches

his nose up like he's in pain, sniffs. "I mean it though, don't tell anyone, she'd kill me. It's a secret she's my gran."

I pull a face for *I really don't care*. Clearly, Mrs Hollowbread isn't just mean, she's fairy-tale evil, refusing her grandson soap or clean clothes. It's the only reason I let him stay walking beside me, despite the screws in my stomach tightening as we approach the metal gates ahead, joining the last dregs of students sloping in late. I reckon this Sam can't much like school either, the way his swinging arms become stiff by his side. I could say something encouraging, I suppose – Old Me would – but The Crack's back in my mind: I'm imagining it swallowing the house up whole, like some giant hungry mouth. By the time I reach my locker, he's gone – I didn't even notice when he left.

These days, this is what I do: I tuck myself into back seats, or by walls, or around that corner in art. I've got really good at finding spots and spaces where I won't get seen. Hard-working, polite and quiet (but don't be a genius), then teachers won't need to think about you. Outside of class, well, I've worked out, if you pin your eyes to the shiny school floor and hum a song in your head, you can practically ignore the fist bumps and selfie squeals; the "weirdo"; "what's her problem?"; "loser".

Like Mum, I wasn't always this way. But you'd need that TARDIS to believe it.

Lunchtime: I hide in the library. The sudden quiet from the corridors is like a breeze on a swelteringly hot day. I like its smell: old paper and the tang of Mr Kowalski's extra strong mints. He used to be a history teacher in Poland. Now he's our librarian. He loves doing both, he once told Asha and me, because all stories are drawn from the past, he said. I go in, passing my fellow sanctuary-seekers, and head straight to the computer desks; hurriedly Google. I'm not sure what I'm hoping for – *all right*, yes, I am – some miracle that The Crack will seal itself magically. My search just comes up with the usual: rainfall will make any hole worse; that crevice in a cliff in Whitby – it's grown. *Landslip worrying residents near West Bay*. That's new. My throat swells as I click on it. West

Bay's just down the coast from us. I scan photos of miserable locals. A picture of crumbled sandstone, like brown sugar, piled on the beach. "*There's nothing for it,*" a council spokesperson is quoted as saying. "*The houses will have to come down.*"

"Need help with anything, Faith?"

I almost leap from my seat. Mr Kowalski. I didn't realise I'd made a noise, but I can feel the space where a groan must have left my mouth.

I quickly shift my body to hide the computer screen and shake my head: "Just more homework." Like I'm your usual, commonplace student. Yeah, Mr Kowalski, you know: School, Insta, Netflix. Not: Mum, Noah, House With Giant Garden Crack.

He adjusts his glasses and smiles like he accepts my answer (I find people prefer to), and I accept the mint he offers me (even though they make my eyes water). I like Mr Kowalski. I like the way he speaks, sounding out every word properly, and the way his curly hair is longer and messier than most male teachers'. I like how he takes notice of every student, staring at your eyes curiously, like everyone's a mini-story to be read. But I suddenly like him a little less when he peers round me and says, "Are you worried about your house, Faith?"

I follow his gaze to the crumbling cliff headline, swallow hard, before turning back with a prepared Hollywood smile. "My house is *fine!*"

Mr Kowalski tilts his head. He's always been interested in The Lookout, trying to talk to me about its history. I used to find it embarrassing in front of my friends. Now I've got no friends to be embarrassed in front of, I still don't want to talk to him about it: I need to make The Lookout as invisible as me.

"My heart is still in Krakow, Faith. I know how important home is!" His kind eyes smile; my back tenses. I'm unsure where this is going. "Do you know I am now part of our town's Preservation Society? It grants money to help preserve local history." He pauses to make a little cough that smells minty. I brace myself. Other People cough around me a lot these days. "In fact, your father..."

*Waaah. Waaah.* It's going off in my head – my "Dad" siren: brash and bold like you get in sci-fi films when they evacuate a spaceship. It started soon after Dad upped and left. When people tried to say things to me. Things with "sorry" noises attached. Things that sounded like they knew what had happened to Dad. When they don't. He'll come back one day, Mum said. And that's all I need to know.

"I've a book ... must read ... next class!" I cut across Mr Kowalski. My heart talking in rapid beats to my feet: *run, get away!* I'm off, fast-walking to the purple beanbag in my favourite hidden corner of shelves; grab any book. That'll do: *1000 Jokes To Make You Laugh*. It won't. I no longer laugh, same as I don't cry any more. My eyes blur over the knock-knock chapter, while my head juggles with cracks, big lies. *"Houses will have to come down."*

A few minutes later, there's a familiar voice nearby.

"Yeah, right, but did you see what he posted back?"

I make a peephole in the bookshelf next to me. Asha and Sian: walking towards the other side of my hideout. Asha's black hair in two plaits; Sian's a frizzy halo around her head. I draw back sharply. If I look at my old friends too long, I get all kinds of feelings in my tummy and up through my chest that I don't like.

"So, just tell him you like him!" Sian says.

Another of Asha's crushes then. I jam my mint between my teeth; Old Me used to be part of those conversations. It's like alien language now. Their voices turn to murmurs as they move along the shelves, before they get closer again.

"Well, I'm giving up on her," Sian's saying. "There's only so many brush-offs I can take."

I suck in my breath.

"My mum and dad want me to keep trying," Asha replies.

A sharp stab in my chest as I picture Asha's parents. I used to eat with them most weeks. I miss Mr Singh's legendary raita and home-baked naans. My mouth waters. I miss Dr Singh checking I was doing OK at science ("We need more girls winning the Nobel prize!"). I even miss watching Asha's twin brothers doing all the things Noah never does. Squabbling over Xbox, flicking snot at each other, forever talking football. I've known Asha and her family since, well, since I remember knowing people.

Their voices start drifting away again.

I sink down further into the beanbag. Like Dad said, if we don't keep fixing The Lookout, rot will set in. Asha and Sian tried talking to me at first. They sent messages too. *Aren't we friends any more? What did I do wrong?* My stomach gripes. It's too late now. The rot's set in. I crunch down hard on my mint, breaking it into tiny pieces. It was all their fault. They *believed* the gossip about Dad getting passed round town like a box of chocolates. Stomach snake snaps at my insides. *Best not to think about it.*

They'll be heading back down the corridor now, linked-arms, heads-close. Joining others, Evie, Nora, Kip at our usual table in the canteen. *Like I care.* I tuck my legs tighter into my body, wishing I could ball up and hibernate forever. I can't really explain why it feels safer not to talk to Asha and Sian any more. I'm just worried about my house.

My school rucksack's crammed, bulging, dragging me backwards with its tins of beans and bottles of milk. My legs ache from the walk to the out-of-town

Tesco. My palms sting from the plastic handles of three "bags for life". I tried and failed to look for that Sam as I left school. I was thinking maybe I could ask his advice on how to get his demon grandmother to back off. But I couldn't see his blue parka anywhere. I'm not sure I'd recognise him without it.

Down St Swithun's yew-lined path; round its jagged-teeth gravestones; through the metal kissing-gate; past Halfpenny Farm with its pink farmhouse, cow smells and sounds; across the field near the disused well that's all sealed up; round the redbrick pillbox, grass growing like hair on its flat roof. I'm always eager for my first sight of The Lookout these days. Like I'm seeing it for the very first time. Its arched door like a mouth. The stone lintel above the windows – its eyebrows. My tower roof, like a stained wizard's hat. *Course*, Vicious Wind decides to blow the second I'm in sight of the cliff edge. Like a nasty dog waiting to welcome me home. It snatches at my "bags for life" and pulls at my hair again. But I won't play. I keep my head down, my body braced, and I concentrate on dinner, and wondering if I can get away with eggs and beans again, and what are our chances of getting scurvy soon if I don't learn to cook better. I don't look up till I'm turning into our drive from the cliff path. Which is when I see it.

My stomach shrivels into a paper ball. There's a shiny black BMW pulled up by our front door. I stare daggers at it. I want to kick it, to push it till it falls – crash – right off the cliff. *How could she!* Mean thoughts about Mum flash across my head. Ones I do my very best *not* to think. *It's her fault Dad left! She kept on at him! Complaining how everything tasted of sea salt. Nagging him to stop "obsessing" over The Lookout! To "give over fixing it up, Ryan!". To move away!*

*It's all your fault!* I shout at Mum inside my head. She's called Uncle Art anyway. When she promised she wouldn't!

# Four

It's deathly quiet in the house when I open the front door. Sometimes I find myself missing the sounds I didn't even notice before. Like Mum singing along (badly) to the radio; Dad's banging, drilling, fixing; Noah being forced to wash up, pots and pans clattering. Talking of Noah, there's his schoolbag, dumped in the middle of the hall; he'll have gone beachcombing before the sky turns black. I'm hoping Uncle Art's beach-bound too, only using our driveway to park, when I catch a strong whiff of aftershave.

Dread creeps up my spine as I trace his scented trail into the lounge. How do I tell him, *I'm not leaving my home*, without my words getting fuddled? I've always been a little afraid of Uncle Art.

I find him crouching on all fours near our oak desk, in the corner behind the tatty purple velvet sofa. Shiny suit. Cropped hair. Two wobbly chins covered by a beard that's more comic book villain than Father Christmas. Polluting the air with that vanilla electronic cigarette of his. Sickly sweet, it mingles with the aftershave and turns my stomach. *I'll never forgive you for this, Mum*, I think, in small, pointy words as Uncle Art spots me. "Faith!"

He clumsily, urgently, starts stuffing paper into an ancient-looking envelope, before fumbling it into a rusty tin box he grabs from the open desk drawer; the box rattles as he stand up. "A little bird told me you've heard from your dad?"

Which is when it hits me. Mum didn't bring him here. *I did!*

"You actually *spoke* to Ryan?" he continues with suspicious eyes. No, "How are you, Faith?" or "Nice to see you, my one and only niece."

I do a Noah, and question him back. "How did you get in, Uncle Art?"

He takes a puff of his e-cigarette, wafting his hand like he's no time for this. "The front door was wide open," he says.

I curse Noah in my head – he never closes it properly.

"*Anyone* could have come in," he adds, tugging his villain's beard with fake concern. "Where's your mother?"

"She's sleeping off a cold," I answer quickly.

"Again?" he says, with a careless sneer. "She's getting lots of colds, according to you." Another puff. "Is she avoiding me?"

"Probably not. Maybe." I'm not sure which answer's better. I'm no good at this. Mum and Dad always dealt with Uncle Art. Vicious Wind whistles through the gaps in the lounge's two sash windows. Enjoying itself. I pull on the frayed cuffs of my blue school jumper. "Who told you about Dad?" I ask quietly. I need him to go. He can't see Mum upstairs. Or the mess in the kitchen. I can't risk him seeing The Crack outside.

"Your Aunty Val's friendly with the receptionist at Noah's school," Uncle Art's saying proudly. "She overheard his teacher talking."

"Course she did," I say under my breath, and I quickly transfer blame on to Mrs Hollowbread.

"When's he back?" Uncle Art's mouth makes the shape of a swear word.

You'd be right to think, *but they're brothers*. Uncle Art should be over the moon at the idea of a reunion! Wrong. He looks like it's the worst thing to happen to him, besides getting his precious BMW scratched. Because Uncle Art would prefer it if Dad never came back. He's just waiting for the right moment to get his hands on The Lookout. With his and Aunty Val's love of beach holidays, new phones, massive TVs, he's greedy for money. That's what Mum and Dad used to joke. I just reckon he's bitter, that Grandpa gave his little brother guardianship of The Lookout over him.

"Very soon," I say, dipping my eyes for Big Fat Lie, take two. "He said he was sorry for leaving without saying goodbye." I stare at my hands, at the three red stripes left by the shopping bags. "He said he just needed space to sort his head out. He's in Scotland. But he'll be home very soon." I'm really hoping Uncle Art didn't watch *EastEnders* the other night, because I lifted every line straight from it. See, TV *can* be useful.

When I look up again, Uncle Art is dragging his tongue across the top of his teeth. I can see his eyes turning mathematical, small black beads in his plump, tanned face. He starts looking round the room, making calculations, taking in the sloping wood-slatted ceiling, the walls bowing like they've overeaten. Till his eyes come full circle to the shelf above the desk. It's where we keep Tom Walker's ancient brass lantern, the one he lit to warn ships of the rocks below. The family tree next to it – I drew that in Year Four. Dad proudly framed it. *Tom Walker, 1731–1798*, is at the very top branch, along with his wife and four children. Tess Walker, his eldest – she's the one whose death Tom stopped time for in our old clock. My eyes move further along the shelf to – *No-ah!* – he's still not replaced the brass telescope!

Uncle Art makes a loud snort up his nose. "So did

your dad ever find the money he was searching for ...
to fix up the house?"

I glance up, meeting his eyes at a slant. Mr Kowalski's
face springs into my head – he mentioned something
about Dad and money too.

"Ryan came to see me just before he ... disappeared,"
Uncle Art breaks off and tugs his villain's beard again.
"Asking to borrow money for this stupid old house!
Convinced he was on the brink of finding some stash
of cash. Like money grows on trees!" His eyes brighten
as if he's imagining that fantasy. "Talking like a mad
man, he was, about the past and that Tom Walker."
He nods at my family tree. "You know anything?"

"I do not," I answer truthfully. I'd not listened to
Dad in a while, especially after he and Mum started
arguing. My stomach snake squirms.

Uncle Art takes an extra-long puff on his
e-cigarette. "My family liked keeping *secrets* from
me," he spits out. His eyes do more sums. "I've been
trying to remember all the hiding places we used as
children. Know of any?"

I shake my head; like I'm going to tell *him*.

He steps forward, making the floor squeak, and flattens down a corner of the rug there with his shoe. "If there's a stash of cash hidden somewhere, I've an equal share of it. You'd let your Uncle Art know, wouldn't you?" He eyes his fingernails casually. "Otherwise, I've a mind to call my mate at the council. Have him lean on someone to do an inspection of the house."

My blood pumps faster. I'm picturing polished shoes congregating around The Crack outside like a funeral burial. I can already see the yellow tape criss-crossing our front door and windows.

"I-I don't know anything about any secrets or money," I say honestly. "And – and you can't do anything to the house until Dad's home!" I stutter; my face is growing hot.

Uncle Art points his e-cigarette at me like he's a teacher. "You know my feelings – I never agreed with your dad about fixing this place up – it's a money pit, wants flogging not fixing! The Lookout's made of good stone. Valuable slate. If this damned house falls, I won't have my inheritance getting scavenged on the beach below."

"We're nowhere near the edge," I repeat what Dad used to shout at Mum.

"No one can predict when a cliff might collapse, Faith," Uncle Art says, in a voice like one of those politicians on the news.

I shake my head frustratedly. Big Fat Lie was supposed to help, not bring Uncle Art round with more threats!

"Look, Val and I have your best interests at heart," Uncle Art adds silkily, lifting his briefcase, as shiny as his suit, on to our desk. A couple of clicks. When he turns around again, that rusty tin box from the desk drawer has disappeared. Words scrabble on to my tongue: *Thief! Stop!* But my throat might as well be plugged with steel wool. I don't know how to stand up to him.

"I'm telling Dad," is all I can eventually come up with, like a snotty four-year-old.

"Don't I deserve some good fortune?!" Uncle Art's spare hand makes a tight fist. "I've waited long enough!"

He locks eyes with me, but Uncle Art doesn't read mini-stories. He glares fiercely, and I want to glare back, unblinking, like in those staring contests I used to have with Asha. I want to show him, he can't treat us like this. But I'm the first to look away. I stare at my feet and pull at my frayed jumper cuffs, until I hear the purr of his precious BMW leaving.

I'm heading for the desk, wondering what was in that ancient envelope and rusty tin box that Uncle Art just stole from us, when I hear footsteps coming – *from below*! I dart into the hall as Noah shoots out, not from the beach but from the cellar door.

"Dad's in Scotland? He's coming back?" His round face is lit up. Brown eyes buzzing. "See, Dads *do* come back!" Noah shouts back down into the cellar, before he adds triumphantly to me, "I knew the sea ghost was wrong!"

My neck stiffens. "You were listening from the cellar?" I purposely ignore the last comment.

"I heard you say Dad called!"

I've not seen Noah look so happy in months, and there's a big part of me that wants to give him the fib as a gift. But then he says, "I'm going to let Mum know!" And I have to make a grab for his sleeve before he can rush up the stairs.

"Noah, no!" I bite my lip. There's a sharp-edged brick lodged in my chest. "It's not true," I tell him slowly. Then I tell him the rest about Mrs Hollowbread and my Big Fat Lie. And I have to watch the light snuff back out of his brown eyes.

"He's not coming back?" he asks, but in a tone that's not a question. "So, the sea ghost *is* right."

I leap on it this time. "There are no *sea ghosts*, Noah! Whoever you talk to in the cellar, it's in your head. They're not real!" I grab his shoulder, forcing his face round to mine. "Noah! Are you even listening?"

His cheeks are wet. "It's you that's not listening!" His watery eyes spark as he shouts back. "The sea ghosts *are* real!"

Which is when I really lose it. "You've got to stop making things up, Noah! *You're* the reason I had to lie in the first place! *You're* why Uncle Art came nosying round! You're going to ruin everything!"

My heart is hammering, but I can't slow down. I've got to keep The Lookout safe. "Do you *want* to leave Mum? Do you *want* to lose our home? Then stop drawing nasty pictures at school!"

Noah's really sobbing now. His face is all bothered and tight.

"The sea ghosts aren't nasty." He pulls at his hair. "The one I talk to, he's looking for lost treasure. And I told him I'm good at finding things!" He takes a watery breath. "I told him Dad was trying to find something too!"

*Dad.* I stab a finger into the air. "That's enough!" I shout back. My whole mouth is trembling. "Stop pretending! Stop acting so weird!" I'm almost screaming. "Be more like other boys! Play Xbox and flick snot and talk football!" I hear Mum creaking above. I spin on my heel. Making quick, rushed strides. The open cellar door is letting out a waft of damp and mould. I never go down there – because Dad said it wasn't safe to go down there, not since he started trying to fix it; he said it was dangerous! I slam it shut quickly. Twist the key in the lock, clenching it so hard my hand hurts, and I shout back at Noah, "You're never going into the cellar again!"

It's all Noah's fault I'm spooked, and hearing things. *Sea ghosts; lost treasure!* I shift position again in bed. I can't sleep, tossing and turning like the angry waves outside. I feel bad. Course I do. I shouldn't have said those things to Noah. I sort of tried to say sorry. But he'd barricaded his bedroom door by the time I'd finished getting tea and making up reasons to Mum why Noah and I were shouting. I didn't tell her about Uncle Art coming round. Or about my Big Fat Lie. Why would I? I don't tell her anything any more. Not about The Crack, about Asha and me not being friends, about how often I go outside, even when the air's like shards of ice against your skin, to check our house is staying put.

I lift my head and thump my pillow into a different shape. The noises get louder with both ears lifted: a sudden sound like a cry. *It's* not *voices!* I remind myself. Old houses talk! Vicious Wind up to its usual tricks, howling and shrieking! The tides, getting sent wild by the moon! My eyes spring open. There's a rattling sound like someone's trying to get out. That'll be *Noah* trying to get *in* the cellar, *stupid*! I pull the duvet over my head, and squeeze my eyes shut. But The Crack's waiting for me inside my head; Suits from the council; Uncle Art stroking his beard knowingly. There's Noah crying; and Mrs Hollowbread telling Mum: Dad's coming home. And then I see him. Faraway and fuzzy, like those scenes in films where fathers return from war – just a dot in the distance that grows bigger until they're there in front of you, solid and real: smelling of soap and stone and sea.

Breathing hard, I tug the duvet down, and snap my eyes wide open; stare hard into the darkness to snuff out everything in my head. When – another noise. Creaking on the staircase this time. *Noah*, creeping downstairs, as usual. Wait – goose pimples erupt on my arms – then how was he rattling the cellar door before? *You imagined it!* I shout inside my head.

A wolf-howl from the wind; a crash from the waves; the house creaks and whines and ticks.

I think about dragging Noah back to bed, but I

reckon he's had his fill of me tonight. I turn over again. I shouldn't have called him weird. Like Finn Dagger and his friends call me. I'll tell him sorry for that. But I won't unlock the cellar door.

I'm not sure when I finally fell asleep. Though the sting in my eyes tells me it can't have been for long. I forgot to pull the blinds on the two porthole windows in my room, and the sun's already forming two buttery shafts, criss-crossing like swords over my bed. The air's freezing though. I daren't put the heating on much. I don't know how long the savings in Mum and Dad's bank account will last for, now Mum's no longer working.

I jump out of bed and get dressed in a chilled rush back into my school uniform. My bedroom's my favourite place in The Lookout. The tower room tucked away under the eaves. Old Mum painted the floorboards white and bought me the rainbow fairy lights across my bed. Dad told me stories of how it was in the tower that, centuries ago, our ancestor Tom Walker would shine the warning lantern at passing ships ("*Why* is it only men who feature in this house's history?" Old Mum complained). Now it's daylight, and I can see my heap of stuffed animals, my books and posters, I could almost laugh out loud – that I came close to believing I heard voices last night. Darkness can do that to you, can't it.

I brush my hair, staring out at the sea from the porthole that looks west, over the orange shingle sand directly below The Lookout. The east porthole looks out towards Cliff Point, which divides Redstone Beach from the sweep of Greystone Beach beyond, with its small pebbles and slate-grey cliff. There's no sea mist or clouds today, just sky as smooth and chlorine-blue as a swimming pool. It makes me feel more hopeful. Like something's lifted. Surely, Uncle Art won't dare call the council now he thinks Dad's returning.

I follow a blue dot moving along the beach. It's Sam, Parka Boy and Evil Teacher's grandson. Out searching again. Maybe I'll distract Noah with helping Sam find what he's looking for. And in return he'll get his gran to leave us alone. I start treading lightly out of the room. Today I'll try and be kinder to Mum. She didn't call Uncle Art after all. And she can't help the way she is. She just misses Dad. Like a barnacle prised from a whale, I think she's drifting without him.

The dinner I left outside Noah's room below is still there, but his door's open and his bed's empty. He must be starving. I prepare my apology as I head downstairs. But Noah's not in the kitchen either. *So what, he'll have headed to the beach early – maybe he'll meet grubby Sam himself.* I think of Sam's infectious laugh and it makes me feel better for some strange reason. I set to packing lunches, sniffing ham that's out of date, tutting Noah (because he's clearly been raiding the food again – the new milk's almost finished!). I can't hear Mum-sounds yet, but I start filling the kettle for her tea anyway; put a slice in the toaster.

I pour an extra-large bowl of Rice Krispies ready for Noah, place it on the table, and I don't think much of it at first – the folded piece of paper propped against the empty fruit bowl, my name scrawled across it. He'll only be telling me why I have to open the cellar again. I reach for it, preparing to decipher Noah's spidery writing. And freeze. Like I've been plunged into the cold sea.

I am running away! I am not coming home till u open the cellar door + let me talk to my ghost! I will ~~foureg fohage~~ forage for my tea so I will not be wanting more eggs + beans thank you NOT very much.

P.S. You are not my MUM u know!

# Five

I am *not* going to worry about him. *Nuh-uh*. Because that's exactly what Noah wants! Make me feel bad; force me to open the cellar door; *believe* his stories about ghosts and lost treasure!

*Lost treasure only exists in books!*

*There's no such thing as ghosts!* I shout even louder in my head, as my mind turns traitor and ponders over those noises last night. I glance up at the sudden creak of floorboard overhead; screw up my face: I'm sick of them both. Here I am trying to keep Other People out of our business and our house safe, and *she's* staying in bed all day and *he's* running around like he's a starring role in *Ghostbusters*! When there's Mrs Hollowbread and Uncle Art waiting for us to slip up. A hotness rises in me, despite the chill in the kitchen. I take big angry strides to the back door. Noah's going to jeopardise everything!

I avoid looking at The Crack as I quickly leave our back garden, turning east towards Cliff Point, to Greystone Beach. It's where Noah mostly combs for what the night-time sea's swept in. I set a fast pace along the cliff edge even though I'm walking straight into a wall of wind. It's not vicious today but it's mean, and its stabbing fingers are soon making my eyes burn and water.

I blink fast, keeping my gaze peeled for Noah below. Since reading *Swallows and Amazons*, he's forever packing his huge explorer's overnight bag to find places to live outside. One summer he mostly slept in the greenhouse ("I like the smell of tomatoes," he said). Old Mum let him; she said explorers need to explore. Right now, explorers need to get to school!

My arms tingle in readiness to grab him and point him to clean underpants and his school bag. Except the beach is deserted. I can't even spot Sam any more.

I go on, past the council sign with its warning of rockfalls and landslips, taking the steps down to the beach. Note: *NOT* the unofficial path made further along by lazy summer tourists. Who don't give a flying fart that you can't grow land like grain and grass! *That my house needs the ground to stay solid!* I throw a nervous glance at what I can still see of The Lookout; roof tiles smeared yellow-grey with lichen. It seems to lean from this angle, as if it's taking a peek over the cliff edge, just like the pastel painting on our many-greats-grandfather clock. I remind myself: *the Tower of Pisa's been standing for centuries!* Then I jump the final step, landing with a round of applause from the pebbles.

"You're up early!"

I jolt upright at the smiling voice. Sam – zipped up and hooded in his parka like it's a cocoon. He must have been just out of sight beneath the rocks.

I'm about to ask if he's seen Noah, when he adds:

"Want to help me find something before school?" He's doing that swingy-jig with his arms again.

"No," I answer bluntly. Well, there's no point sugar-coating it. It's not my fault the arm-swinging halts.

"Oh." Sam pushes his hood off and the mean wind lifts his messy brown hair like it's playing puppet master. "I'm looking for stuff that's worth something."

I push out a long breath – he *is* another cliff-chipper. "You won't find fossils here," I lie.

"Nah, I mean precious stuff. See over there," Sam sniffs and points over to Cliff Point. It juts out into the sea, ending with a profile that looks like a human face, or a horse head if you're Noah (though Noah and I both agree the rocks stretching out far into the waves beyond are a long lion's paw). "In the town museum it says loads of ships got wrecked—"

"Fake news." I quickly stop him there. I shake my head. "My house was built to *warn* ships about Cliff Point," I signal proudly in the direction of The Lookout. "There weren't *loads* of shipwrecks." I make an *end-of* nod. These days, I don't like to think of anything crashing into the rocks near home, even centuries ago.

Sam continues anyway, clearly mistaking my seriously uninterested tone for mild enthusiasm. "...museum says there was smuggling as well. Sometimes precious stuff washes up on the beach!"

"You don't want to believe everything you read," I say wisely. "Besides, *no one* goes to that museum any more." *Well*, it's true. It's not *my* fault Sam's face does a dance like Noah when he gets told off.

He starts kicking at a piece of driftwood. "I just need to find summat dead valuable to pay my gran for food and stuff, you know."

"You're serious?" Aha, I was right then – Mrs Hollowbread *is* fairy-tale evil. I see Sam in his dirty, ragged clothes, brushing cinders from the fire. "You *pay* your gran to take care of you?"

"No one does nowt for owt." Sam shoves his hands under his armpits and sniffs again. "That's what me mum says."

I follow his eyes out to where the tide is rattling stones like arcade pennies.

"Where is your mum anyway?"

"Err…" Sam frowns like he can't remember. "London," he finally says, going pink.

"You don't sound from London."

Sam rubs his neck. I suppose I could ask other questions, about why he's moved here and stuff, but I'm not on the beach to make friends. *Remember? You don't talk to Other People.* Other People only make everything more complicated. Ask nosy questions; push their beaks in; talk and laugh about you behind your back. Besides, The Lookout's calling for me. I've not drawn Mum's curtains yet or given her breakfast. I start heading back up the steps.

"Maybe after school then?" Sam calls from behind me. "If we find owt precious, we can share it!"

I know the arms are back swinging without looking, but I don't answer. By the time I reach the top, he's disappeared again.

I manage to get to school with enough time to go to the library first, even after all my chores: Mum's tea and toast; my lunchbox and Noah's (even though he doesn't deserve it). Old Mum used to write scribbled notes with our lunches, with smiley faces and messages like "you're my favourite daughter" and "missing you already". So, I wrote one for Noah, ordering him, "don't let anyone see you!" and "you're for it when I catch you!" With two *grumpy* faces.

I feel a little calmer just by closing the library door on all the corridor noise and elbow-pushing that I never used to notice back before Dad upped and left. I pass Mr Kowalski refereeing a group of Year Sevens fighting over the last copy of *The Hunger Games*, and quickly claim the same computer as yesterday (because lately, I sort of feel safer when things stay the same).

I log on to Mum's email. We've never had Wi-Fi at home, it's never reached the cliffs, which Dad always said was a good thing and Mum always argued was yet another reason to move away. It makes my insides squirm with anger at her again, and I start banging out her absent message to Noah's school using a haughty voice that's not even hers. I decide on Noah having *"proper bad"* vomiting and diarrhoea, because they actually *insist* you stay off for that (just in case he's still playing *Swallows and Amazons* tomorrow). I press send before anyone can look over my shoulder.

Mr Kowalski is getting the book-fighting Year Sevens to shake hands now. His curly hair is pulled back in a man-bun today. I think again of what Uncle Art said. That Dad told him he was going to find "a stash of cash". My breath shortens. I *could* just ask.

"Good morning, Faith!"

*I daren't ask.* I stare down at my shoes, smeared with wet sand.

Mr Kowalski makes a sound like he's struggling to put words in the right order. "I heard in the staffroom this morning ... that your father is coming home?"

I glance up. "Was it on Twitter?" I mean to say it as a joke, but my voice comes out like ice cracking.

"You must be very relieved?" Mr Kowalski's kind eyes peer into mine, like I'm a mini-story. Every blink turning the pages in my head.

Reading my Big Fat Lie.

"Dads *do* come back," I murmur, thinking of what Noah's imaginary ghost said to him. I start walking – *go!* – before my "Dad" siren can start. Casually – *like*

*I've not a care in the world.*

"Faith, one moment!" Except Mr Kowalski only goes and follows me, doesn't he, out into the noise of the corridor.

My eyes dart. Speaking to school staff out here is a sure way to get attention. I already spot Finn Dagger and his mates nudging one another, pointing. I suddenly want to be with Noah, safe at home.

"Maybe you and your father can think about what I said yesterday," Mr Kowalski continues, as a herd of older students storm past like it's feeding time at Halfpenny Farm.

Mr Kowalski pushes his mint across his mouth. Behind his glasses, his kind eyes must read I didn't listen yesterday, because he adds softly, "Your father enquired at The Preservation Society about funding to restore your house. But he never made an application," his Adam's apple bobs, "before he left." We both duck as one boy whacks his rucksack at another.

"I walk past your house sometimes. I can see there is work urgently needed."

Now there's a lump like an Adam's apple in my throat.

"The Lookout is part of this coastline's history," Mr Kowalski says more excitedly.

"It is," I reply cautiously. "The Lookout warned ships, so they didn't crash." It feels good to share my pride in my house.

"Then your house deserves to be preserved, yes?"

"Preserved?" Exhausted butterflies cause a faint tickly feeling in my tummy. I think it might be hope. I imagine wire netting preventing the cliff from falling. Concrete pouring into The Crack. Uncle Art being forced to admit defeat! I flinch as the morning bell goes. A teacher bellows, "Get to class!" down the corridor.

I pinch my hands together. "How do I get this funding?" I say, carefully, like I'm taking tiny steps across a tightrope.

"I believe your father was advised to gather proof of The Lookout's history. Did he start this?"

I make a nod that's halfway between yes and no. Like I said, I zoned out from Dad this past year. The snake in my stomach hisses. *You stopped listening!*

*Because he was always hidden away, usually in the cellar, fixing, banging, drilling!* I answer myself. That's *if he wasn't arguing with Mum! No wonder I spent more and more time at Asha's and Sian's!*

Mr Kowalski's eyes are following mine closely again; I can't give too much away. It might bring Mr Kowalski to the house too. I blink; and say quietly, precisely, "I'll get proof."

"Maybe I can help you with this?" Mr Kowalski's kind eyes shine. "We can dig around together!"

I step away from the wall, shaking my head briskly. No *digging*, thank you, *interfering*. "That's OK, Mr Kowalski," I say politely. There is no "we". There's just me. "My dad is coming back, remember?"

I reckon the next time I look in the mirror, I'll have grown a nose as long as Pinocchio's.

# Six

I slam the soles of my shoes against the pavement, quickly putting distance between me and school. Through the church and into the field; Halfpenny Farm smells heavy with manure. Dad was on a mission to mend our house. I already knew that. I frown, thinking again of what Uncle Art said about Dad asking to borrow money from him. I just didn't know how desperate he'd become. So why didn't he apply for this funding? I pick up my pace, round the disused well. Well, I'll do it for him. Another picture forms in my mind, this time sunshine-framed, with Mr Kowalski passing me one of those giant lottery winner cheques. We'll be in the local newspaper and on social media, and then Dad will see it wherever he is, and he'll come home, because he'll know: we saved The Lookout!

I approach the redbrick pillbox with its head of grass hair, the salty sea air filling my nose and throat; a brisk, biting wind sweeping in my other worries: Mum, Noah; Mrs Hollowbread. I've got to entice Noah back inside, *without* opening the cellar door. When our hamster, Oasis (RIP), escaped under the floorboards, we'd leave a trail of carrot and lettuce back into his cage. Maybe I can trail Noah's favourite chocolate Hobnobs through the garden, into the kitchen. Pretend not to notice him, till he's inside, and – slam – lock all the doors! A rare laugh bubbles inside of me, popping as quickly as it comes, right as I hear—

"School all right?"

It's like he's just magicked himself from thin air again. His parka's still zipped up to his neck like a sleeping bag, even though it's a little warmer today.

I cast around, to see where he came from – there's only the pillbox nearby.

"You shouldn't go in there," I tell him archly. It was another place Dad said not to go, soon after he banned us from the cellar. "It's unsafe," he told us, "you don't know what you'll find," with a face that seemed to say giant rats or an escaped prisoner. I stride on past Sam to the cliff path. Now I have The Lookout in my sights, I'm eager to get home: Hobnob trail for Noah; check on Mum; dig around for proof of The Lookout's history for Mr Kowalski. A spark of hope zaps through me again, like my bones have been buzzed in "Operation".

"Want to see what I found?" Sam catches up with me.

"Sorry, busy." I slice a curt hand through the wind, hoping he can read sign language for "get lost".

Clearly not. "I found them on the beach," he shoots in front of me, opening his grubby palm to reveal two small ammonites. "Cool, huh? Reckon I'll get paid lots for them?"

I look from the fossils to Sam. His free arm is doing

a solo jig, so I decide not to tell him *everyone* finds ammonites, that the fossil shop in town sells them for a pound. "Maybe," I say instead and stride on. Regrettably, Sam keeps up with me. Hasn't he got *other* friends?

"I'm still looking for shipwreck booty on the beach though; to get well rich!"

I glance across at him, to see if he's joking. There's a smear of dirt across one cheek and his lips look chapped. Mrs Hollowbread must make him wash in bird-bath water. After she's got him to sweep her chimneys and pay for his supper.

The arm-jig speeds up. "There's this one massive shipwreck, right – the museum says it was called *Providence*. An' it was bringing jewels and gold coins and stuff and then – smash – it lost it all to the sea!" Jiggy-arm goes frantic, then stops abruptly. "Along with all its crew."

"I know," I say airily. I vaguely remember doing the *Providence* shipwreck in primary school.

"Then d'you know your house is mentioned?!"

I stop walking, pushing my hair back from the

wind's games. "The Lookout's in the town museum?"

Both Sam's arms do a jig now. "It is! A dead small picture! Blink and you'll miss it!"

I stare over at the stained roof and bowing walls of my house. Maybe the museum can help with evidence for Mr Kowalski's funding. I've plenty of time before I need to start cooking my speciality eggs-and-beans again. "Is it open now?" I try to say it in a way that doesn't imply I'm keen. But Sam's eyes light up all the same.

"Two till four, Tuesdays, *Thursdays* and Saturdays! Let's go!" he says and spins one of his ammonites in the air like a lucky coin, before I'm able to tell him he's not invited.

The museum's on the first floor of an ancient Tudor building on Market Square. I've not been up here for years; to be honest, I didn't know it was still going. Mum and Dad used to bring us on rainy days when we were little; now everyone goes to the big "History Centre" in Exeter.

Sam smiles, "Welcome!" as we enter, like it's his

home he's brought me to. He's been prattling excitedly the whole way, about some reconstruction – "This wicked Victorian pharmacy! It's got crazy quack cures and dead weird tonics and powders!"

You'd think we're going to the best funfair ever, not some dreary museum that smells of wet carpet and isn't good enough for school trips any more. There's not an interactive button in sight.

"Isn't it brilliant!" Sam says gleefully, taking in the gloom.

"Hmm," I reply vaguely. Really, I've never seen anyone so excited by a dark warren of disorderly glass cabinets filled with mounds of musty, dusty, old objects. The floorboards here creak worse than The Lookout.

"There's never any staff around," Sam says, "Or visitors." He grins, like he likes it that way. Which is at least one thing we have in common.

"It's down here," he continues, pausing to nod fondly at "School!" – a display of old-fashioned class photographs and equipment (a nasty looking cane). "I love owt Victorian," Sam says dreamily. I hurry him on. There are no windows, and it's getting swelteringly hot in the small aisles. I'm not surprised that even Sam starts to unzip that grubby parka of his, but I am surprised at the red T-shirt underneath. "Did you not go to school today?"

Sam's eyes shoot down to where his uniform should be.

"Like I'm going to tell on you!" I almost laugh, thinking of Noah. Because Sam's expression is like I've discovered a kidnapped baby bear under his parka. (What if fairy-tale-evil Mrs Hollowbread is keeping him off school?) I try and soften my voice. "So, what, you come from London, but you support Manchester United?" I tick my head at his red chest and the yellow emblem there.

Sam frowns. "Loads in London support Man United," he says defensively, his face flushing as red as his top, and he quickly zips up the parka again, even though he must be roasting.

*Not your problem*, I remind myself.

"You're right: blink and miss it," I say dryly, as we reach a shadowy corner of the museum and a small cabinet crowded with naval memorabilia, from caps to medals. There's a shelf with a dusty, old model of a ship, with miniature wooden details, little cream-coloured sails and rigging, and even tiny painted sailors on-board.

"*Providence!*" Sam stabs a finger at the glass, leaving a dirty mark. He proudly reads aloud from the information board in old-style type next to the ship.

"*The galleon,* Providence, *was bringing a chest of gold coins to Devon, along with other precious goods: jewels, teas, spices, and silks. It hit the rocks in the very early hours of 6th April 1770 near Cliff Point, shattering the hull into pieces.*"

I stiffen, imagining it.

"*You can still find shards of wood from the ship washed up on shore today and, if you're lucky, other precious items. While some of the jewels were uncovered, the chest of gold coins was never found,*" Sam continues, not even looking at the text now. *Just how often does he come here?*

"*Did the gold sink with* Providence? *Or did*

smugglers, common along the coast, steal the wreck's spoils? We might never know. All of the crew drowned," Sam finishes sadly.

I peer closer at the miniature sailors on the ship. Those drawings of Noah's are suddenly swirling round my head, the ones that Mrs Hollowbread showed me. Eyes bulging; distorted features; hair swimming about their heads. Noah's *imaginary* sea ghosts ... with *imaginary* lost treasure ... did Noah draw them ... *drowning*?

I shake my head. *So, what if he did? Noah will have been here himself! Or done the* Providence *topic in school too!*

"And there's your house!" Sam stabs the glass again with another dirty fingerprint. I move along the cabinet, squinting my eyes at a tiny old pencil etching. He's right, it's The Lookout. I recognise the walls, windows, my tower room. The only difference is it's set further back from the cliff edge.

My breath slows – on the sea below, *Providence* strikes the lion's paw of rocks beyond Cliff Point. I press my nose to the glass to read the typed note next to it. *"With no lighthouse on this stretch of coast, domestic houses like The Lookout usually lit lanterns to warn passing ships of dangerous rocks below."*

*Usually?* I jerk away like the glass has smashed. "It's not The Lookout's fault it couldn't save *Providence*!"

Sam makes a puzzled face. "Who's saying it is?"

"The Lookout *saved* ships," I say tightly. I fumble in my rucksack for my phone to take photos for proof. I only use it to check the time these days. It's not like I need to talk to anyone. I take some shots, before staring again at the model ship. Noah's drawings are haunting my head. The heat starts to feel suffocating. I tug at my school shirt. "I have to go."

"But you've not seen the Victorian pharmacy yet!" Sam's voice is disappointed; he blocks my way out, digging into his parka pockets. "I'm going to give one of these to my gran later," he says, holding out his two ammonites again, like they're just as precious as any lost gold coin.

"You can have the other one, to buy food and milk and stuff."

My eyes narrow, picturing those gossiping parents in The Teapot. "What makes you think I need money for food?" My voice comes out high-pitched. I've let him get too close. "I don't need *anything*," I say, "or *anyone*," I add, to make it clear: I'm not his friend.

*Noah!* He's still not back inside when I get home. But I've got to see to Mum first. She won't have eaten any lunch as usual. I frantically search the kitchen cupboards (which Noah's raided *again*!) for what else I can add to eggs and beans that might make her eat more.

The house squeaks as I carefully climb the stairs with Mum's dinner tray, as if it's commenting on my addition of a treat size Milky Way I found at the back of the fridge. "Old Mum used to love chocolate," I tell its walls defensively, before: "Dinnertime!" I switch to bright and breezy, like I'm in *Call the Midwife*.

Mum's lying on her back, eyes to the ceiling. Perfectly still, as if she's one of those stone effigies you see in old churches. I purposefully clang the tray down on her bedside; she lets out a surprised gasp and swiftly turns from stone effigy into elderly woman, stiff and creaky as she sits up. Her hair *really* needs a wash, and there's an eggy stain on Dad's pyjama top. I find it hard to keep my smile.

"Oooh, yum," Mum says in her feathery, fragile voice, but she doesn't make any attempt to eat. Not even the Milky Way. "Where's Noah?" she adds. "He didn't say goodbye this morning."

I stay in *Call the Midwife*: jolly laugh, *ho ho ho.* "He's helping some boy find what he's lost on the beach!" I lie, *jollily.* My eyes catch sight of Dad's bedside table – beneath his reading glasses: *Dorset Wreckers* – extra "proof" for Mr Kowalski? I make a hurried dash for it. Lingering too long on "Dad's side" always gives me a pain in my chest.

I cradle the book in one arm, like it's a piece of Dad himself. "Mu-um," I start cautiously – because I've got to ask. "Did Dad ever talk to you about gettingmoneyforthehouse?" Finishing fast, with another *ho ho ho* jolly laugh – I don't want to panic her.

Which is just what I do. It must be the forbidden

word, the bolt of electricity that jolts through her.

"About getting funding to fix The Lookout?" I repeat more brightly, minus the "Dad" word.

"Fun," Mum says faintly.

Which is ironic, because I think she's forgotten what that means, till I realise: "*Funding*! Yes!" I say, relieved; and I'm back picturing The Lookout all polished and sparkling, The Crack filled, cliff edge strengthened. That is till Mum makes a strange moan of a noise, more elderly animal than elderly woman now, and her eyes seem to become as wild as one of Noah's drawings. "The funding wasn't enough. He wanted more. I shouted at him to stop. I did." She jerks her neck like she's struggling to swallow something.

It scares me; my stomach snake squirms. I shouldn't have mentioned Dad. It upsets her too much.

"It's OK, forget it!" I say hurriedly, and I start prattling cheerfully, Sam-style (the weather, "eat your eggs and beans", "ooh look, Milky Way!"), while I dance round tucking her sheet into her mattress (*Call the Midwife* hospital corners). I make a fast retreat, with this morning's mug of cold tea, sprinting down the stairs even though it makes The Lookout scream and whine. There's something about Mum awake and speaking that sometimes makes me more nervous than Mum asleep and silent. Sometimes, I think I'd prefer her like Sleeping Beauty. Hair washed and brushed, waiting there peacefully for Dad to come and kiss her back to life.

# Seven

"No-aah! Where are you?" I shout loudly from the edge of our garden, scouting the coast both ways. There's a pale grey mist hanging over the sea that's laced with pink from the sun setting in the west. I might find it pretty if The Crack wasn't looming like a monster's open mouth behind me (*wider? longer?*). If Mum's feathery, fragile words weren't gripping my shoulders like a hungry bear. "The funding wasn't enough. He wanted more." *More?* I jump at a disparaging gull noise from above. Out-squawk it: "Noah!

Come inside!"

Nothing. My shoulders slump. It's not just Mr Kowalski's funding news I want to share with him. I suddenly want my little brother back badly. It's only been a day without him, but I'm already missing his freckled face and stuck-up red hair. I even miss watching him drift in and out of Planet Noah.

I press Dad's book tightly against my chest. "I know you've raided those chocolate Hobnobs, Noah!" I bellow into the wet sea air. "Come back or I'll never buy them again!" As threats go it's not my best.

"And... And I'll clear your room out!" *Better.* "I mean it! I'll put your whole stinking room into the bin!" I roar – when out of the corner of my eye I catch a flash of blue and grey streaking out from the side of the house. *Got him!*

I storm after him as he ducks inside the greenhouse. It's in the far corner of the garden – that didn't used to be the far corner till last year's landslip. There's a warm blast of summer and soil as I push on the glass door. I don't like going inside. It only reminds me I've let Dad's tomatoes die.

"What're you playing at?" I swallow back other cross words. *Treat him gently, like Oasis, our ex-hamster.*

"You can't camp in here. It's too close to the cliff edge."

"The cliff won't fall for ages," Noah throws my words back at me. "And I'm staying here till you unlock the cellar door!" He crosses his arms and presses his lips together. If he was standing, he'd probably stomp his foot – he looks that stubborn and determined.

I sigh and look around. There's a sleeping bag and his big overnight explorer bag and a leftover crust from the sandwich I made him this morning. There's shells and stones and ... more of those drawings of his. I take a deep breath like Old Mum used to when she was trying to make us do something, like wear another jumper or eat one more forkful of broccoli. "I know you've read about the shipwreck, *Providence*, at the town museum."

Noah pulls a blank face. "Our town's got a museum?"

I frown at him. "You've learnt about it at school then."

Noah's face goes blanker.

"Well, why else are you drawing pictures of *drowning* sailors?" I stutter.

"Because," Noah says in a "duh" voice. "My sea ghost told me he was in a shipwreck."

"*Providence?*"

Noah nods and bottom-shuffles towards a drawing on the ground. "That's *him*. That's who I've been talking to," he says defensively.

I bend to get a closer look. Noah's drawn a boy who doesn't look much older than me; bulging eyeballs; rising hair; old-fashioned sailor clothes. His hands reaching out like he wants pulling out of the picture.

"This is what your 'ghost' looks like?" I say. My chest is becoming wheezy and tight. Ghosts. Do. Not. Exist.

"Maybe." Noah stares down and picks at his worn trainers. "The light doesn't work in the cellar and he won't let me use my torch." Bottom lip. "He doesn't want me to see him."

Noah must hear the roll of my eyes because his own flash fierce again. "I've drawn what he's told me he's like. He says the other sea ghosts are scared! That's why I can't go too far into the cellar."

"Bit convenient," I murmur under my breath.

Noah's face becomes more stone-like. "My ghost screams at night. I know you've heard him too! You're lying!"

"It's the wind howling, Noah!"

From stone to rock. "Don't believe me then! But unlock the door. I have to give him something." He starts rustling through his carpet of drawings before brandishing a piece of paper, like a golden ticket. "I told him I saw Dad exploring, before he upped and left. With a secret map. My ghost said to copy it."

I shake my head. "Now what are you on about?" The smell of decaying tomatoes is getting worse.

"Dad had a map. He pretended he didn't when I asked. But I saw it! It was old and yellow and had symbols on it! I drew it best I could."

"Show me!" I demand, putting my hand out for it, already hearing Mum saying Dad wanted "more". My eyes squint at a few random crosses, a felt-tip pint of beer and a steeple, a wavy line for the sea. I hand Noah back his "map". It's as much use as shiny toilet paper. I've no time for childish games – Uncle Art will soon realise I lied about Dad's phone call, and he'll come back with his mate from the council! I must get the Mr Kowalski money. Fill in The Crack. Fix the house. And then Dad will—

Noah's bottom lip is wobbling like he's about to cry again. "I want Dad to come home," he finishes the sentence in my head; his voice a mouse-squeak.

"It'll be all right," I say. When nothing feels all right. I push a hand down to pull him up, but he plants his trainers far apart, like he's taking root.

"I told you, I'm sleeping in here till you open the cellar door."

*Stay calm.* "Fine, I'll think about it." I steal one of Old Mum's phrases.

"Promise?"

"Promise," I fib. Hamster tactics, remember?

"But visit Mum and have tea." I swallow like adults do, with purpose, extending my neck, to show him I know best. "And go to school tomorrow. *And* change your underpants!" I throw back, stepping out into the garden. The air's cold in contrast to the greenhouse and the pink-rimmed mist's been erased by a dark grey sky. I keep Dad's *Dorset Wreckers* book tight against my chest. I'll put it back soon. Dad needs everything the way he left it. Careful steps round The Crack. Disparaging Gull is on the roof now, beady-eyeing me. I glare back – seagulls hate eye contact – and glimpse a shadowy figure in Mum's bedroom window. Thoughts of ghosts make my heart beat rapidly, till I get closer and realise – it's Mum herself. When she's never out of bed, except to visit the bathroom. I try to catch her eyes, but they're fixed on the sea. She's urgently searching for something in the water. I follow her gaze. The sea is flat, like a huge grey blanket; empty.

# Eight

*"Find home!!!"*

I wake with a start at a distant scream, my breath coming in short, quick gasps. *It was a dream!*

"Find home!!!"

*Not a dream!*

I grip the edge of the duvet. Not Mum's voice. Noah? I stare hard into the dark shadows dancing round my bedroom. My stomach snake is sliding up my chest, making it hard to breathe. It's gone quiet. Just the usual noises: waves crashing; wind howling; the wood beams creaking; pipes clanging. That's Mum snoring softly below. I fumble for my bedside light, switch it on, before I swing out of bed, padding bare feet on cold floor to my west porthole. Behind the blind, a full moon lights the sea in a silvery-white. I peer round the roof to find the greenhouse: soft yellow orb; shadowy shape – Noah and his torch. He's returned to camp there! I glance at my open bedroom door. My snake expands in my throat. If Noah's in the greenhouse, then who...? Breathing harder, I make a grab for my dressing gown – I must've imagined it: *I must have!* Another noise below. I freeze like I'm playing party statues. The distinctive cat whine of the cellar door. Footsteps!

I edge back, ice-cold water sliding under my skin. Footsteps in the hall below! I wait, holding my breath to hear, ears straining like they're Harry Potter-extendable. My heart is going to burst out of my ribcage, it's pounding that hard. *Whine* and *click* – the sound of the cellar door shutting again.

I picture the ghost-boy from Noah's drawing. I throw off my dressing gown and dive back into bed, covers over my head. Squeeze eyes shut, stick fingers in ears. *You're imagining it!*

"Ca-ca, ca-ca!"

I wake again, this time to the sound of another gull mocking me from the roof. The fog in my head and the sting in my eyes confirm I hardly slept at all. I was on alert, half-awake for more noises the whole night. *There are no sea ghosts in our cellar!* I tell myself again for the millionth time, as I hurriedly get dressed. *Just more games from Noah, trying to spook me, to make me believe his stories and unlock the cellar door. See! I forgot the advice of that library pamphlet: I gave him a "platform"!*

I continue morning duties. Passing the cellar door downstairs, I quickly rattle the knob. Still locked. Check the key is still in the secret pocket in my school rucksack. It is. OK, so Noah *somehow* found another key to the cellar. Made his voice deeper, older. I nod my head decisively. I. Do. Not. Believe. In. Ghosts. But I do believe Noah raided the cupboards overnight! There are breadcrumbs and empty packaging on the counter. "Tesco again," I grumble, pouring out Noah's breakfast. I take it to the greenhouse across damp grass, round The Crack (*is it wider?*), along with his school uniform. Except Noah's not there.

"Off finding again!" I snap at the decaying tomato plants. Spying that daft "map" of his, I angrily scoop it up, crumpling it in my fist.

"I'll just eat this, shall I!" I tell the salty air outside, shovelling Rice Krispies into my uneasy stomach as I speed back indoors and shove the map in the kitchen bin, with a satisfyingly loud whack of the lid. Before I take Mum her doorstep toast and milky tea, extra sugar.

I almost slop it all over myself, I halt so sharply in her bedroom doorway. She's standing by the window again. If I'd not heard her snoring last night, I'd think she'd been there all the time. She's dressed too: tracksuit bottoms and Dad's navy blue woollen jumper, the one that always smelled of sea and sun even after it was washed.

I put the tray on her bed. "Are you going out?" I say slowly, half-pleased, half-horrified at the thought.

She doesn't answer. Instead she does a Noah: a question for a question.

"Did I see him out there?" she says. I notice her eyes urgently following the waves again.

"You might have," I say cautiously. "Noah's out exploring."

Mum turns to me slowly, her brow making shapes as if I'm not making sense. "Noah?" she says. As if Noah wasn't who she meant. My snake pokes his head through the pile of Krispies. I hurry out again.

Nope, no sign of Noah anywhere! I walk with angry yet sluggish steps to school. Stomach fiery; eyes sleep-sore. If Noah doesn't get back to school soon, he's going to get us found out! Just when I might have found a way to fix the house, keep Uncle Art off our backs ... and get Dad home!

I turn off the cliff path. Pass the pillbox – which reminds me, I've not done my homework on the Battle of Britain. (*Sir, an imaginary sea ghost ate my homework?*) Pass the disused well. Pass Halfpenny Farm, where the cows are moo-ing noisily from the milking shed. By the time I pass the church, its clock reminds me I've left it too late to use the library computers. *Damn you, Noah, a million times!* I tug my phone out as I walk past The Teapot; sneakily log on to its Wi-Fi and quickly send another email from Mum to Noah's school.

If life was normal, if I was going back home, to dump my bag in the hall like Noah and land at the kitchen table to be served a snack and to be asked about school by Old Mum or Dad, I'd probably answer that it was an "OK day". What with my history teacher giving me a homework extension (a dad upping-and-leaving gets you special privileges it seems); what with it being sunny enough to spend lunchtime in that hidden corner of trees behind the playing field.

By the home bell, I know for sure I imagined last night's noises. The house's voice has all kinds of twists and turns. Doesn't Dad always say, the rooms echo with centuries-old footfall; the stone walls store the breath of past lives? I head to the library, hoping the museum photos and Dad's *Dorset Wreckers* are good enough as "proof".

Mr Kowalski is stacking books but he spots me hovering behind him straight away, like he's got kind eyes in the back of his head as well as the front.

His kind front eyes smile. "Just the student I always like to see!"

I dip my head. I'd rather not be seen. "I have proof about the history of our house, for the money," I mumble, shrug. "I went to the town museum."

"The town museum? Oh, I always forget about that place!" Mr Kowalski says with a wink.

"I think everyone does," I say, and we share an eye-smile this time and it almost feels like a normal exchange with someone for the first time in months. Which is maybe why the butterflies in my tummy grow less tired: we're going to get money for The Lookout. Suddenly, in my head, I'm running down a train platform into Dad's arms; you know, like Bobbie at the end of *The Railway Children*. Those three children made everything better and *their* Dad came back!

"Well, this is great! Share with me what you have

found and then The Preservation Society will make an appointment for an assessment."

Pins and needles break out all over my body. I step back. "An assessment?"

"Yes, to see what work The Lookout needs."

I make a jerk of my head. They'll see Mum, that's what they'll see. They'll see Mum needs work, and beds need making and bins need emptying. They'll see Noah running round like a wild thing with his overnight explorer bag! "Actually –" My voice comes out too high. I clear my throat. "Maybe I might wait for Dad to come back first."

Mr Kowalski makes a face like I've just said I'm waiting for the tooth fairy. He pushes out a hand towards me. "Why not let me help," he says. At least I think he does. I move so fast, there's no chance he can follow me this time.

*Stupid, stupid, stupid!* I repeat angrily to myself, with each stomp across the school grounds. *Of course The Preservation Society would want to see The Lookout for themselves! Other People want to poke around! Pick our house apart! Interfere –* I stop abruptly, spying their shoes by the school gates: Sian's DMs with the purple laces and Asha's black ballet pumps. I look up, instantly clashing eyes with them both.

"All right, Faith," Sian says.

I've not been this near them since we stopped talking. "The Three Amigos", we used to call our group chat. I thought it was impossible for there to be a universe where we weren't friends. Asha and me especially. Now, I don't even recognise her. Well, I mean, I do: shiny black hair; long face; serious brown eyes. But she's not the same best friend I spent virtually every minute with, FaceTiming, shopping, sharing our favourite milkshake (candyfloss, extra cream, sprinkles). She's not her any more. Because I'm not me.

"Hi, Faith," Asha murmurs, not-quite-looking at me. I not-quite-look at her back.

Sian scratches her neck and says, "Finn Dagger's telling everyone your dad called."

*More gossiping.* My stomach curdles – it takes me back there in a flash. To the moment we stopped being friends. The day after the police – a Him and Her in black-and-blue uniforms – arrived at our door, soon after Dad upped and left. Him and Her in Blue told us they'd found our boat, broken and battered down the coast. And straight away, the town began greedily passing round their chocolate box of gossip. Even though Mum told Him and Her in Blue that the boat had been on the beach for ages!

"The sea must've taken it; it grabs things if you're not looking!" she said!

"For goodness' sake, Ryan would never sail in a storm!" she said!

"He left in the night on foot!" she said!

"He's not missing; he just needs time!" she said!

And I said the same to Asha and Sian, that very next day.

But they wouldn't listen. I could tell that from the shuffling of their feet; their awkward glances at one another. Like I was the one making-up! Asha – my best-friend-in-the-whole-world-Asha – would rather believe Other People's *lies*! Click-of-fingers-fast, our friendship slipped over the edge. As swiftly as our old garden fence fell off the cliff.

"What's-not, hey?" not-quite-looking Asha softly breaks the silence. It's our old secret code word from primary school, when we wanted to tell each other not to worry.

A sudden bitter taste appears in my mouth. *She's only talking to you because her mum and dad told her to!* I say nothing. I walk away. Fast.

I take the alleyway behind the high street. Because Asha and Sian won't be far behind – Friday afternoon means a milkshake at The Teapot. It's not the snake, but something heavy and slug-like that fills my insides. *Like I want a milkshake in The Teapot anyway!* I don't like to go where people know me. That's why I'm about to walk the mile to the big Tesco out of town rather than go to the local Co-op – after Sheila with the tight perm who works there asked, "I've not seen your mum lately, Faith?" with that noise at the end like she was demanding an explanation. No one knows me at the big Tesco as *the girl in that house.*

I'm coming out the other end of the alleyway, joining the bottom of the high street, when my heart makes a funny leap. I can see Sam across the road, same grubby parka and more frown lines than usual. For someone who doesn't want to be around Other People, I'm weirdly pleased to see him. Now I can't get Mr Kowalski's funding, maybe I'll scour the beach with him after all. What if the museum is right and there is a chance of finding precious stuff? I start to wave, following his eyes to where he's staring uncertainly; jerk my hand down again. The curved, broad body of his gran, Mrs Hollowbread, loading shopping bags into a cream-coloured Mini (clearly Sam has to stand twenty paces behind her!). I move briskly.

Too late.

"Noah's sister!" I hear Mrs Hollowbread call across the road. "I want to talk to you!"

*No; no talking.* I don't stop. I move faster, darting into a run, taking a right down Pressgang Passage, my footsteps echoing off the walls, a left, a right, past The Ship Inn, until I finally rejoin the main road leading out of town, on my way to St Swithun's. I'll leave Tesco till tomorrow.

I feel better as soon as I can see the crayon line

of blue-grey sea in the distance. It looks so still, but I know as I get closer, I'll see the waves rising and curling and thrashing towards the shore. I'm thinking maybe most things look calm until you get up close, when there's a screech along the pavement beside me. Mrs Hollowbread pulls the cream Mini up so close the tyres squeak against the kerb, the wing mirror almost slicing off my elbow. I come to a jaw-dropping standstill.

"I'm a teacher." She winds down the window. "When someone runs, I know they're guilty."

# Nine

"I think I'll visit your mother after all," she snaps, small bursts of spittle firing out through the open window. "Get in."

"But I'm not allowed to go in cars with strangers!" – is all I can come up with.

"You *know* who I am, for goodness' sake!" Mrs Hollowbread leans across to open the passenger door.

I could still refuse, I'm sure it's my right; I could threaten her with police action for a nearly-severed left elbow. But I can't have her getting to the house before me! I walk to the open door like I'm Anne

Boleyn approaching the executioner's block, and tuck my legs, stiff with dread, into the small car. Flick a look to the empty backseat – Sam can't have wanted in on his gran's nasty witch hunt.

Mrs Hollowbread pulls away. I squeeze my hands tightly between my knees and remind myself: you've *one* job – protect The Lookout, at all costs.

One of those Christmas tree air fresheners swings from the rear-view mirror: the mix of pine and petrol is nauseating. I clear my throat. "Thing is, Mum's got Noah's lurgy."

Mrs Hollowbread makes suspicious slits of her eyes, releasing a horse-snort of a noise for *a likely story*.

"It's a plague house right now," I continue. "You'll be dancing with death."

Another horse-snort. "And what particular plague is that? *Puking* and *poo*?" She says the last few words like she's mimicking me.

My stomach tightens. I try to remember what I wrote in those emails.

"The school receptionist and I agree, most women your mother's age don't favour a 'vomiting' emoji when they record their child as absent."

I send evil thoughts to that school receptionist. She's clearly got it in for me too.

"Also, you cannot *'literally die'*," she adds with a huff. "You're either dying or you're not." Like she's giving me an English lesson.

I pinch my hands tighter between my legs, because I swear otherwise I'll reach across for the steering wheel and veer the car back to the kerb, like I used to steal the dodgem wheel from Dad when he got bump-happy. The memory of whizzing around with him at the local fair suddenly turns into a flashing neon sign in my head, unusually loud and clear: *Come home, Dad!* Because I don't know how else I'm going to get out of this one.

There's a silence as hard as rock between me and Mrs Hollowbread by the time our feet crunch across our gravel driveway. My hands have gone numb from being squeezed between my legs and my heart's thudding like I'm one of those First World War soldiers preparing to go over the trenches. I fumble for my front door key, conscious of The Lookout's window-eyes above, sorrowful and surprised that I'm bringing home this vampire (well, she looks like she can bite). Maybe she won't be able to cross our threshold if I don't invite her in! The tap of her sensible shoes against the hall tiles soon answers that one.

"What is that stench?" she says, wrinkling her long nose.

I sniff the air. You don't usually notice your own house smell, do you? But truth is, the house probably does stink. The kitchen bin needs emptying. And there's Mum's musty sheets and Noah's aquarium-bedroom. There's the whiff of damp and mould that creeps up from the cellar.

It gives me an idea. "Yeah, that'll be Mum and Noah. Like I said: it's the worst *diarrhoea* I've *ever* known." I waft a hand in front of my nose.

Mrs Hollowbread flinches.

It just might work. "You should see the state of our toilet!" I imagine the most disgusting loo ever, so it's pictured on my face. "Do you have any tips for getting brown stains out of white sheets?"

Mrs Hollowbread's throat convulses; she covers her

mouth with her palm. *Result!* "Maybe I should phone instead," she's saying, backing towards the front door. *Yes!* Turning to go!

She stops.

We spot it at the same time.

"Not too poorly to draw his horror pictures then?"

Noah's stuck that drawing of his boy ghost on the back of the front door. Now there's a speech bubble from the boy's mouth in purple felt tip: *"Find my treasure so I can go home!"*

My palms become clammy. I can hear Noah's stubborn voice in the words he's scrawled below.

Cos u will not open the ~~sellah~~ cellar I am off 2 find his treasure 4 him. So the sea ghosts can go home!

"The fever ... Noah's delirious," I murmur frantically.

Mrs Hollowbread's eyes have shrunk back to paper slits. "Sea ghosts? Off to find treasure?" She lets out a long exhale and rubs her temples. "Please tell your mother I'm here to see her."

"Mum! What're you doing?"

Great! She's up again! The one day I actually *need* her under the covers! She's standing in the exact same position at the window as this morning, her eyes fixed on the sea. This morning's toast is curling untouched on her bedside table.

"Mum, I need your help," I whisper urgently to her, tugging at her sleeve – Dad's favourite jumper. I suppose at least she looks the part of being ill: her skin is as grey as the unlit room; there are new black smudges under her eyes.

I try and tell her about nasty, interfering teachers that we need to keep away, but she's not *listening*. "Mum, *please!*"

She lets out a small moan. "He's out there," she says to the window glass. Her pupils growing large as black pebbles.

"Yes, he is – Noah's just off exploring, but don't tell *her* that, OK?" I take a short, sharp breath. "Tell her: Dad is coming home."

The black pebbles swell into discs, like ink dropped

in water. "They've found him?" She turns to me, each word like it's her last breath.

*Never say the "Dad" word!* "No, he's not, it's –" I glance back to the door, picturing Mrs Hollowbread tapping a sensible shoe impatiently downstairs. "Have a bath!" I change tactics. "You don't want to talk to Other People, do you," I tell her, not ask her, as I start to marshal her out of the room; quickly, quietly along the landing, and into the bathroom. "Run the water like you always do!" I hiss. "You're our only hope!" I say, going all Star Wars, and shut the door on her panicked, grey face.

Next, I rush into Noah's bedroom. "Ah, he's still asleep!" I say loudly for the benefit of Mrs Hollowbread below. I close the curtains to turn the room to night-time, before I work on his bed.

"Really – what *is* going on here?"

I fly slap bang into Mrs Hollowbread as I come out, arriving at the top of the staircase. Her eyes fire insults as she stares around. My own follow: peeling paint; the island-shaped stain on the ceiling; lacy cobwebs in every corner; balls of dust like tumbleweed across the wooden floor. She runs a finger down a hairline crack next to the stairs. "This place looks like it's falling apart at the seams!"

"It is *not*!" I say, the insult making my tone bolder than I'd usually dare use with an adult that's not Mum or Dad. "The Lookout's been here for three hundred years." I lift my chin. "It'll stay put for another three hundred!"

Mrs Hollowbread makes a critical puff noise between her lips. "I'm sure you can agree, it needs a good tidy and clean." She indicates the bucket that collects water leaks; the pile of dirty clothes I've not yet taken down to wash.

"My dad says there's no worse waste of time than cleaning," I answer decisively with this new bold tone.

Mrs Hollowbread sighs and shakes her head. "But your father isn't here is he, Faith?"

She may as well have taken a knife out of a sheath and pushed it into me.

"He's coming," I say, but my bold tone's gone limp.

Something streaks across her miserable eyes. It looks like sympathy – it won't be. "Where's your mother, child?"

A pause; the house ticks and sighs, then – "In the bath!" I say victoriously, at the sound of running water from the bathroom. "And probably on the loo, *again*," I add for extra measure.

Mrs Hollowbread covers her mouth. "Oh, this really isn't good. Where's Noah? In here?" She doesn't even wait to be shown. The mean old interfering bag just barges past me, making my floorboards shriek like she's taking pleasure in hurting them with her ugly sensibles, straight into Noah's room, fixing those vampire eyes on the long uneven lump in Noah's bed.

"He's sleeping!" I plead. Any second now, I can see it's all about to come down on my head: Mrs Hollowbread will pull back the duvet to reveal the mountain of cuddly toys I piled into a small duvet-human shape just moments ago. I see social services taking Noah away. The council making us leave. The Lookout being handed over to Uncle Art for its stone and slate, for flogging, not fixing.

My snake invites its mates round to party in my stomach, while Mrs Hollowbread steps gingerly round a tangled mess of sandy shells and *Explorer* magazines on the floor. It's all been for nothing! Getting Noah to school on time, cooking eggs and beans every night, keeping Mum's forever-sleeping a secret.

"Noah, can I talk to you?" Mrs Hollowbread reaches a hand out to Big Bear and Raggedy Rabbit.

My snake party grows wilder. I *must* protect The Lookout! *At all costs.* An elastic band snaps somewhere in my head. "I know you're mean to Sam!" I shriek, making her jump back like I've slapped her. I can't quite believe I've actually spoken those words to a teacher. *But she's a witch who's evil to her grandson! And she must leave!* I take a deep breath like I'm winding myself up. "You come round here to check on Noah, when you don't even let Sam go to school, or wash!"

Mrs Hollowbread's eyes are growing so wide I think they're going to pop out of their sockets like one of Noah's sea ghost drawings. She stumbles, putting a hand out to the wall like she's about to faint. "Why are you talking about Samuel? How do you know about Samuel?" She sounds like she's in pain.

I wring my hands, trying not to get distracted by the distraught look on her face. (*It's only because she's been found out!*) I reload my weaponry. "He's told me how you treat him, that—"

*Crash!* There's a horrendous noise from below. Like the sea has barged its way through the front door. Followed fast by a voice, low and menacing: *"Find my treasure!"*

We stare, big-eyed, at one another – until we're both chasing out of the room, on to the landing, down the stairs. Mrs Hollowbread's breath is as heavy as mine as we come to a standstill in the hall: our many-greats-grandfather clock is lying face down on the floor like a felled tree.

"Who else is here?"

I shake my head in answer, and bend to touch the clock, like it's an injured person. A fan of shattered glass is spreading out across the hall tiles. *It can't be Noah*, I'm thinking, my chest filling with a watery fear. The clock is heavy – my little brother couldn't reach high enough to push it over! Besides, that was *definitely not* Noah's voice. I slowly lift my eyes from the clock and follow another sound down the dimly-lit hall. The cellar door is open, banging lightly in its frame. I try and gulp back the ball of cotton wool that's expanding rapidly in my throat, to tell Mrs Hollowbread what I suddenly realise must be true: "We have ghosts."

Noah's been right all the time. A night-time scream, *"Find home,"* echoes through the distant corners of my head. I've not been imagining it.

I look fixedly at Mrs Hollowbread. "We have sea ghosts in our cellar."

# Ten

She's gone. I wanted her to tell me what to do. (Get a priest? Find a medium? Call Ghostbusters?) Instead, she claimed I was making it all up! Like Noah and I are no better than Bash Street Kids playing daft practical jokes on her. All she seemed bothered about was Sam!

"H-how do you even kn-know Samuel?" she said again as she left, looking more vampire-like with the blood drained from her old skin.

"There's a ghost in my house!" I replied, because she can't have heard, otherwise she'd listen!

But soon after, the tyres of her Mini were screeching – she couldn't get away quickly enough. Though not before she'd put her witch-curse on me: "Your *mother* must bring Noah to school on Monday. Or I'll forward my concerns to social services."

The clock's way too heavy for me to lift alone, so I just brush up the broken glass into the kitchen bin and shove the whole smelly bag into the black wheelie outside. Before I remember to shout up the stairs to Mum: "You can go back to bed now." Adding: "You don't have diarrhoea," because sometimes I think Mum hasn't got a thought of her own in her head any more.

Only then do I turn back to stare at the open cellar door, still gently banging in its frame. Even the snake party pauses to consider it. I've been working so hard to keep people from getting into The Lookout – when all along, there's been a bigger danger already inside.

The floor seems to tilt and sway under my feet like it's suddenly made of water.

*The Lookout is haunted.*

I force an into-battle breath. Retrieve the cellar key from my rucksack. Charge forwards, like it's a weapon – and lock the door. *Again*. Now what?

I could shout, "I believe you, Noah!" into the grey, sea air? I turn back round slowly, to the sea ghost drawing stuck to the front door: *"Find my treasure so I can go home!"*

Noah said he saw Dad with a map. "Stash of cash." (Uncle Art.) "More." (Mum.) I blink hard. *A treasure map?*

A new purpose ignites like a flare in my chest. I flick a daring look to whatever ghost is lurking behind my cellar door – any treasure belongs to The Lookout! – and turn determinedly in the direction of the lounge. I head straight for the oak desk behind our tatty purple sofa, with the shelf above – Tom Walker's old lantern; the framed family tree I drew in Year Four; Tom's telescope that *should* complete the line-up (Noah!). I imagine him searching for treasure through it (*ahoy there!*), and I rapidly yank open desk drawers. I've got to race my own brother to find lost gold coins. I rifle through piles of papers, for clues, a map! Trying not to think of scary sea ghosts plotting beneath my feet.

A few minutes later and all I've come up with are tons of estimates from builders and plasterers and stonemasons. Figures with lots of zeros at the end, for all kinds of fixing that needs doing. I see Dad at the desk, when I came home from Asha's or Sian's, sitting here till late, clutching at his hair with both hands. The constant arguing with Old Mum: "It's all you think about, Ryan! This blasted house!" I glance up angrily at her room: *it wasn't his fault!*

I slam my hands back on the desk and inhale deeply – something pungent shoots up my nose. Uncle Art's aftershave! In a flash I hear the noise of his shiny briefcase being clasped shut; that rusty tin box disappearing from the desk. His silky voice: "Trying to remember the hiding places." He was here searching for Dad's secrets; like a smuggler himself!

I'm off, darting around the room, checking all our hidey holes: the loose brick in the wall above the fireplace – gold! Well, the foil kind from an egg. (The Lookout always serves up the best Easter egg hunts.) The hollow space beneath the window seat.

Only Noah's shell stash. I stare back to the desk, remembering Uncle Art straightening the rug with his shoe: the cracked tile! I rush over and drop to the floor. Pulling the old rug back, I press on the broken tile till half comes loose, revealing the hole beneath. I pat my hand around, nothing but dust – whatever he found has gone now. I sit back on my legs. I'm thinking of more hidey holes to search, when my eyes spy something papery against the skirting board. It must have fallen down the back of the desk, when Uncle Art was stealing in a hurry.

I reach for it carefully; it looks stiff yet fragile. A funny shade of yellow, with old-fashioned flowery writing that's even harder to read than Noah's. The words start mid-sentence at the top – it looks like the last page of a letter.

...not benefit from the suffering of others for ill-gotten gains. I know you are desperate, but these are desperate times for everyone, Father. It is not worth the loss of our values, our home, our family!

*Oh, Father, I want you home so we might speak in person. I am frightened, but I must go now. If I do not return, remember, I tried to right your wrongs.*

*Your affectionate daughter, Tess.*

My eyes hurry to the family tree on the shelf above. Up its wonky oak to the top: *Tess* – the eldest daughter of Tom Walker. The dead daughter who Tom Walker "stopped time" for! Sealing up our many-greats grandfather clock. I don't need to calculate the dates I've listed neatly below the names to know how long she lived. I always felt sad about my ancestor Tess dying when she was only seventeen, even if Old Mum explained people's lives were perilous back then. Wait a second – I get up to peer closer at my younger writing – "Died: 6th April 1770". My breath arrives faster: at the museum, that was the exact same date of the *Providence* shipwreck!

My mind zips, like I'm in a high-hedged maze, trying to find the centre.

Was Tess Walker's death *connected* to the

*Providence* shipwreck?

What does she mean by "ill-gotten gains" and "right your wrongs"?

I need the rest of the letter. I nod my head determinedly. And I know who has it.

I brush the dust off my hands and go and tuck the old letter safely in Dad's book, *Dorset Wreckers,* in my rucksack. It's quiet in the hall, but the hairs on my neck still rise at the thought of what's lurking below.

"Stay in your room!" I shout up to Mum (*like she'll go anywhere else*) as I grab my coat. I leap over the fallen clock and shoot through the front door as quickly as you can say "Mrs Hollowbread's an evil coward." For the first time in an age, I'm actually relieved to be leaving my house.

I cross our drive to the garage and fiercely drag my bike out from beneath a jumble of wheels, purposely ignoring the boat-shaped gap next to our old blue Volvo.

The sun's getting lower, casting crystals across a flat sea as afternoon turns evening. I take a cursory look along the coast for a small red head, before I jump on to the saddle and start pedalling, fast, as if the ghosts are chasing me, chains clanging; I must find this treasure first. I pedal so fast I'm wheezing by the time I reach the bus station on the far side of town. Hurriedly lock my bike against a lamppost as the number 44 to the big town pulls in. Twenty minutes later and I'm standing outside Uncle Art and Aunty Val's house. It's the same Lego-brick beige as every house on their neat estate, with matching conifer pots like border guards either side of their front door. Their porch has no lacy cobwebs, no ugly cracks. They always insist visitors remove and carry their shoes.

I take a deep breath and ring the bell.

"Why, Faith!" Aunty Val opens the door, letting out a burst of too-hot air (Aunty Val doesn't believe in climate change). She's busy with a tea towel and smells of furniture polish and hairspray; her made-up eyes give my dusty school shoes a grimace. She's reluctant to invite me in; not that you'd know it if you were passing. "How wonderful to see you!" she beams. "I love how you don't care what you look like!"

Old Mum said Aunty Val "gives out criticism like compliments", to make her feel better about herself.

"Is Uncle Art in?" I reply stiffly.

"He is," she says, but still doesn't invite me in. She clip-clops away in her heels (*she's* allowed shoes indoors) and I hear some urgent whispering in the background, before the clip-clops are replaced with the shuffle of Uncle Art's slippers (he's *not* allowed shoes indoors).

I lick my lips, readying the opener I've practised the whole bus journey here, to scoop the truth out of him like Hercule Poirot with a fishing net. I spent last summer reading Agatha Christie (you get through a lot of books when your house doesn't get Wi-Fi), whilst Dad was busy fixing and Old Mum was busy arguing. But when Uncle Art fills the doorway with a blunt, "What is it, Faith?" I blow it with a nervous, "You s-stole a t-tin b-box!" More Penfold than Poirot.

"Who do you think you are?" he barks, waving his e-cigarette, before taking a fierce vanilla-scented puff. "Coming to my door with childish accusations!"

Now I'm a practising liar, it's easier to spot other

people's fibs. And Uncle Art just told a mammoth one. I can tell from the faint red tinge to his tanned cheeks, the way his left eye gets a slight twitch. He has the rest of the letter; maybe even the treasure map. I grit my teeth, trying to urge my eyes to fix on him not the left conifer plant. "You took an old letter," I tell the evergreen.

"Oooh, call the constable: an old letter!"

I move one eye sideways. A flush is rising up his neck. He scratches at it. Another nervous puff of vanilla.

"I spoke with Dad again." *If you're going to tell a lie, make it a big one, right?* "He says you're to give that tin box back to me," I add breezily, like I'm simply collecting charity for a jumble sale.

Uncle Art sucks at the beard hair beneath his bottom lip. "You know people are saying you made it all up, about your dad calling?"

Now my face starts to burn. *Deep breath.* "The treasure map too, please."

"There's a map?" A dark cloud passes across Uncle Art's face. "Everything in that house is half mine, you hear? If there's a map—"

"It's Dad's! Dad's the guardian of The Lookout, not you!" my voice shakes. He doesn't have it.

"Yeah and look where it's got him. Obsessed, just like my parents before him. He learnt it all from them, how to get fixated on fixing. Soon as they inherited that house, I never saw them. Did they care when I got bullied at school? *No.* Were they there to visit me when I had my appendix out? *Forgot.* In the audience when I graduated? *Not likely.*"

I open, then close my mouth. Aunty Val twitches their lounge lace curtains.

"It cost my dad his whole pension to keep mending that house." Uncle Art's neck is turning red as sunburn. "You want to know how much inheritance I got?" He stabs his chest. "Nada! Big fat zero! Your dad and I had to dig into our pockets to pay for the bloody funeral!" He growls the last sentence, but his eyes suddenly look wet. It's probably the breeze in the air. I can't imagine Uncle Art even possesses tear ducts.

I bunch my hands and I take a gamble. "I know you're searching for treasure," I say quietly.

"*Searching?*" Uncle Art makes a condescending face. "I don't need to *search*. Once my mate at the council visits, it'll just be a matter of time before they condemn The Lookout."

The Crack looms massive and angry in my mind.

"Then I uncover all its dirty secrets. Easy!"

"I won't let you!" My face is getting hotter. "You're a thief!"

Uncle Art starts laughing, big throaty bellows. "But we're descended from thieves, Faith!" He points his e-cigarette directly at me, like the worst kind of teacher. "That ancestor of ours who built The Lookout?"

"Tom Walker?" I swallow cautiously.

"That's him. He was an old rascal according to this old letter you want so badly. Caused some ship called *Providence* to crash. Was a 'wrecker', it says. I went on Wikipedia," he adds grandly, like he's consulted with the wiseman. "You should take a look." He assesses me sideways then blows out his chest like a general. "Our family, Faith – were *wreckers*!"

And he slams the door in my face.

# Eleven

I'm not sure how long I've been sitting on the bus. I don't even realise it has wheezed back into the station, till the bus driver's face appears in front of mine. "Last stop, love! Unless you want going back there?"

I shake my head, I do *not*. I replace *Dorset Wreckers* in my rucksack and step down into the sounds and sights of the bus station, like I've emerged from underwater. The thrum of buses pulling in and out; workers rushing to get home; old people talking loudly to one another.

The whole bus journey I've been lost in Dad's book. I've been with sailors in old-fashioned uniforms, shrieking and scrambling to escape the sinking *Providence*. I've been living the lives of "wreckers" – Dorset smugglers who took thieving one deadly step further, "wrecking" ships. Shining their lanterns on cliffs near rocks to force ships to crash for easy looting. Using their lightkeeper roles to get rich!

According to Uncle Art – that's what my ancestor did! He forced *Providence* to crash, and all the crew to die, to plunder its treasure! Tom Walker, who built The Lookout and used *my* room to *warn* and *save* ships – was a *wrecker*!

*This* must be what Tess Walker meant by "ill-gotten gains" in her letter!

A heavy weight lands on my chest, making it hard to breathe: that means Noah's sea ghosts are here to reclaim treasure – from the family who *stole* it from them in the first place! From the family that caused their deaths. My skin turns icy-cold under my winter coat.

*No wonder the sea ghost I heard today sounds*

*furious! No wonder he screams at night!* My thoughts spin like a merry-go-round.

*If it belongs to them, they should have it!*

*But they're ghosts! It's not like they can open a bank account!*

*The Lookout needs the treasure! Dad needs to come home!*

*But... What will the sea ghosts do ... if the murderous Walkers steal it again?*

I start weaving fast round snaking bus queues, trying to remember where I locked up my bike. I'm so tense with worry and confusion, I don't even spot him at first. Standing with his back to me, checking a bus timetable, with the kind of bag over his shoulder like he's going somewhere, for a long time. For some daft reason, that makes me feel worse.

"You're leaving?" I come up behind, not meaning to startle him.

There's no crooked-teeth smile, only a thin line with a scowl. "I'm not talking to you." He turns back to the timetable.

"What have I done?" I ask in a small voice.

Sam pushes a hand up like he's stopping traffic but doesn't turn to face me. "You promised you wouldn't say anything about me living with my gran!"

"I haven't!" I say quickly.

His eyes swipe round. The thin line's a sneer now. "You told my gran she's mean to me! And now I have to leave!"

I flush red with shame. "Mrs Hollowbread told you what I said?"

"You told her she wasn't letting me wash!"

"Well," I dance my head and try to subtly indicate his grubby appearance.

"She's not horrid to me." Sam swipes under his nose furiously. His eyes look small and pink. "You don't know what you're talking about. You shouldn't have said anything! How'd you like it if I told my gran about your brother!"

My neck stiffens. "What about him?" I spit out. "Noah's ill in bed!" and I storm away as if there's tiny powered rockets beneath my feet. Because clearly, I can't trust Sam after all – he's loyal to his vampire gran even if she's chucked him out! *Why should I even mind if he leaves! See, this is what Other People do! You let them in and they let you down.* I find the lamppost with my bike and start unlocking it with clumsy fingers.

"You're a liar!"

Sam's beside me again.

I pull my bike lock away angrily. "I am *not*!" I ... lie. My breath comes hard through my nostrils as I wait for him to say it – that he also knows I made it up about Dad coming home.

But instead he says, "Your brother's not ill. I saw him a couple of hours ago! Big bag and rope." He pauses for breath, his last two words sounding more concerned than cross.

"Rope? Where?" I ask urgently. *Has Noah already found the treasure?*

"Apologise first."

I narrow my eyes. "For what?"

Sam lifts a brow and starts counting off on his fingers. "For saying what you said to my gran. For being unfriendly. For being shouty. For..." He shakes his head. "Three things are enough."

"Where did you see Noah?" I say. That weight on my chest is getting heavier. I've got to talk with Noah, before he hands over gold coins to a gang of sea spectres. "All right, I'm sorry," I add hurriedly.

Sam's looking pointedly at the darkening sky.

I droop my shoulders. "I'm *very* sorry."

He makes a brisk nod. "I saw him walking across the churchyard – with a bag the size of him."

Noah's overnight explorer bag. "How did you know it was him?" I frown.

"I've seen him around," Sam says quickly, and flushes.

I've no time to wonder why he's embarrassed. "Can you show me?" I say quickly.

Sam pinches his mouth and stares round at the bus station, back at me. "All right; I've not got enough money for the bus fare anyway." He shrugs. "Or dinner," he explains when his stomach lets out a rumble so loud I can hear it above the engine noises around us.

"Treasure? You're telling me there really *is* ... buried

treasure?" Sam asks, his mouth wide open and stuffed full of sausage roll. I gave him money to buy one for each of us from the Co-op.

"I think so," I say, and take a bite from mine to stop myself adding, "ghost treasure!" For all I know his gran's already told him about my spectral "prank". And I don't want to scare him away. It's a weird relief telling Sam about my ancestor "wrecking" *Providence*.

"There." Sam halts as we enter St Swithun's yew-lined path. "I saw Noah walking round them old graves."

I scan the higgledy-piggledy stones in the far corner of the churchyard. The light's dimming into a fuzzy grey. There's no sign of him now.

Sam wipes his mouth with the back of his hand, leaving a trail of grease. "So, you reckon this Tess girl did summat?"

I rest my bike against a gnarled yew tree. "She was trying to 'right' her dad's wrongs." I carefully pull out the last page of Tess's letter and hold it up for Sam to read because his fingers still look greasy.

"She ain't happy with her dad, is she?" Sam blows out his cheeks. "Don't blame her from what you just said about him."

I put the letter safely back. "My uncle has the rest. And he seems to think the treasure must be at The Lookout." I pause, thinking of Noah exploring. "But my brother's convinced there's a treasure map that goes beyond the house."

Sam's arms get jiggier. "Sounds to me like we should follow your brother!"

"Follow him," I repeat, picturing Noah, his face almost as grubby as Sam's, no clean underpants and armed with rope and his massive explorer bag. My stomach clenches. "I'm supposed to be looking after him," I say aloud. "He's only ten, and he's small for his age." I knead my eyes as they start to sting. I won't cry. "I've treated him no better than our hamster, Oasis."

"A hamster called Oasis? Cool. That's my favourite band."

"My mum's too," I say distractedly. *Mum.* Behind us, the church clock strikes seven. *It's getting dark and she's alone ... in the house ... with angry ghosts.* "I need to get home." I grab my bike and race it back towards the gate.

"What's wrong?" Sam keeps up with me. "I'll help you find Noah and the treasure!"

I glance frantically at him. *Fine.* "Thetreasure-belongstoghostsinourcellar," I admit, in a fast stream of words.

I wait for Sam to start his infectious laugh; or to say, "Ghosts? don't be bloody stupid!" Or to tell me some story (because *everyone* has a ghost story) about seeing some blurry figure at the end of his bed (because it's *always* at the end of beds). *Or* to make a quick getaway like his cowardly gran.

But he says nothing. He stares into the sausage roll bag, like he's sad about it being empty.

I push on the gate. "I said, there are ghosts in our cellar!"

Sam coughs like something's stuck in his throat. "I don't reckon ghosts exist." He rubs his upper arm with his free hand. Wrinkles his nose. "It'll be a trick probably."

"No! I've heard them. Really! They're shipwrecked sailors from *Providence* and Noah's finding their treasure for them. Which is probably the right thing. But our house needs the money!" I add, more impatiently than I mean. But Sam's making me feel stupid for believing in ghosts now.

"You could always share the treasure?" Sam looks hopeful, before he frowns and scratches his neck. "Except – there are no ghosts." He takes a deep breath and crumples his paper bag into a ball.

"Seeing is believing. I bet I can prove to you they're not real." He lifts his chin heroically, though his blue eyes still look sausage-roll sad. "See what's *really* in your cellar."

"Err, yeah, *ghosts*?! And a particularly angry one who forced our old clock over!"

Sam makes a strange "oh" noise.

"Well, ghosts don't scare me," he states, matter of fact. "Alive people scare me more." His eyes seem to get even sadder. "Like me mum's boyfriend."

I frown with him. I'm not sure what to say to that.

"I'm not brave enough to meet a real ghost," I reply eventually.

"How can you know what you're brave about till you've done it?" Sam inhales long and hard through his nose. "Just take my word for it. There are no ghosts." He nods convincingly then smiles, all crooked teeth and left dimple. "Let's go to the cellar."

# Twelve

Sam's the first person I've invited home in a long while. Which makes me think briefly of Asha and Sian and how we'd come back from school and race up to my tower room to chat in secret. I never walked softly up the stairs then. "You're like a herd of elephants!" Dad would call after us. "Remember, this house is ancient!"

I never did remember, until looking after it became my job.

"I'm sorry," Sam says when he sees our many-greats-grandfather clock lying across the floor; another "oh" noise catching in his throat.

"Not like it's your fault." I make a face at him. "It never told the time anyway," I add, because he still looks upset.

We lift the clock together. It takes us several tries, it's that heavy. "All the glass is broken," Sam says in a pained, small voice when it's back against the wall. Only a few glass shards remain on the clockface. Without it the pastel painting of the house and the ship seems brighter, more vivid. I push my fingers out and trace the carved T.W. and X on the wooden door and think again of Tom Walker stopping time when Tess died. The very same day he "wrecked" *Providence*. How *did Tess die*? I'm thinking, when I catch Sam staring over my shoulder, like *he's* seen a ghost.

"I can't."

No. He's just seen Mum.

"I can't," she repeats again. Sitting halfway up the staircase, in Dad's old jumper, cradling the cordless phone in her lap. With a look on her face like she's not sure how she got there.

"Who are you calling, Mum?" *Not Uncle Art; please not Uncle Art.*

Her hands start wringing the phone like it's plasticine. "He's *gone*, isn't he?"

"Noah's just out exploring, I told you," I say loudly, like she's hard of hearing.

But she's not listening. She's looking right through me. She bunches a fist and pummels it into her forehead. "I saw him, I did ... on the beach."

"Noah?" Sam says.

She doesn't answer him either; we might as well not be there. *What must Sam be thinking? First, my tales of ghosts, now this.* I sprint lightly up the stairs, pulling Mum up. She weighs nothing compared to the clock. Quickly, I lead her back to her room, chattering about dinner to distract her, because eggs and beans are the only way I know how to talk to her now.

"How do you know it's that one?" I say, when I come back downstairs and Sam's waiting at the cellar door.

"Is your mum all right?" he asks back. "Does she need a doctor?"

"She's fine!" I say, my voice coming out too high. I'm starting to regret letting Sam in. Seeing Mum like that; questions like these are *exactly* why I keep Other People away.

I fetch the cellar key from my rucksack before I can change my mind; quickly swipe my phone torch and unlock the door. Drawing back against the waft of cellar-damp and mould, ready for an onslaught of sea ghosts, dripping with salty water and covered in seaweed like in *Pirates of the Caribbean*. "*Find my treasure!*"

But only the house speaks; its usual ticks and whines and creaks.

Sam rounds me and starts descending.

"Wait, the light's broken!" I call after him.

"I eat lots of carrots," he calls back and disappears into the dark.

I take a deep breath and put one foot on to the steep wooden staircase. Dad said not to go down – it was unsafe. His renovations were making it dangerous, loose bricks and toxic dust, he said. I gulp back something hard and sharp in my throat. *I don't want to*. I start descending. If my little brother can talk to the *Pirates of the Caribbean*, so can I. Besides, I can't leave Sam to face them alone. He's helping me, even after I dropped him in it with his gran.

Another step, and another; down the creaky, flimsy wooden stairs. The smell of damp and mould gets stronger. My phone torch is rubbish; shadows jump and dance round me. "No!" I leap off the last step as something hard presses against my arm. I spin my phone round, expecting an octopus head with seaweed hair and a ghostly weapon.

"It's just me!" Sam appears in my phone light, holding a giant torch of Dad's. "Here, take it!" He pushes it into my hands.

"See? No ghosts here," he says brightly, as I gratefully shine a stronger light round the room, taking timid steps towards the long worktable. It's cluttered with familiar tools, a broken toaster, tangles of old wires, and ... empty food wrappers? Cheese ... and crackers ... and Cheerios! *Ghosts don't eat!* I snort through my nose: Noah's kitchen raids! Beneath the table, I toe what looks like a sleeping bag. *Ghosts don't sleep!* He's been sleeping in here as well as the greenhouse!

A ghost-sized weight lifts from my chest.

"Only us humans!" Sam echoes this new revelation.

"You're right!" I say. I could almost laugh, except something's still niggling at the pit of my stomach: how did Noah get another key to the cellar? How did he push over the clock; transform his voice? I circle Dad's torch round the back of the room, searching for more evidence of my little brother's spectral tricks. "Look!" My torch hand freezes.

The walls. Thick black fractures, lines, growing like tree branches – I stare up – disappearing into the ceiling above. I gulp cold, damp air, picturing them spreading out under the soil above like a giant worm. Forcing The Crack to appear and split our garden in two. I go and press my hand to the stone; soggy plaster crumbles off in my fingers, revealing more holes and cracks beneath. The heavy weight returns, squashing my chest. Is this what Dad was trying to fix? All those builders' estimates in the desk. Is our house splitting apart from *below*?

"Yeah, I know. The walls are cracking like an eggshell," Sam says solemnly behind me, as if he's seen it before. "I reckon I know what's caused it, too. There's something else you've got to see." He sighs uneasily.

I swing Dad's torch on to the back of his parka. "How come you know so much?" I ask, as he disappears into the room beyond, what used to be the coal bunker. I follow him, repeating my question, when – "What is that?" I gasp.

Sam's shifting an old cabinet away from the wall, exposing a small man-sized hole behind. I can hear the sea coming through it like I'm inside a conch shell.

"*Renovating*, Dad said," I whisper. *More like excavating! Gutting!* All of a sudden, I hear it – an echo of Dad-noises from down here, the ones that sent Mum crazy: chipping and chiseling; banging and drilling. I never asked what he was up to; just asking made Mum stress. I preferred to drink candyfloss milkshakes with my friends, hang out at their houses with Wi-Fi and Asha's dad's legendary raita.

I go over, crouching by the hole, pointing my torch inside. "Could this have made the cracks in the walls?" I ask Sam. *Did Dad hurt our house?*

"Maybe. Was your dad planning to put you down here?" Sam's voice shakes, like he's actually serious.

"What? No! Of course not," I half-laugh. "Why would he do that?"

Sam lets out a noise from the back of his throat that makes me think of what he said earlier, in the churchyard.

"Did your mum's boyfriend," I ask cautiously, "do stuff like that?"

His eyebrows knit together. "He was dead mean." He sniffs and bobs down alongside me. "They're tunnels, see?"

I dip the torchlight further inside. He's right – two tunnels, in opposite directions, just big enough to crawl through on your tummy. Except the one with sea-noises looks sealed up.

"They're both dead ends," Sam says before I can speculate where the right tunnel goes.

"How do you know so much?" I say tightly.

"I go to the town library on Saturdays, when it's busy, so no one sees me, and I've read books, right, about how there used to be secret smugglers' tunnels round here. Government taxes meant people had no choice 'cept to smuggle." Excitement is creeping back into his voice, like this is a game and we've turned history-explorers.

"What if *Providence*'s lost gold coins are buried in the blocked-up tunnels!" His arms are back jigging. "Noah saw your dad with a map, and—"

"Wait…" I blink slowly. I'm thinking I must've misheard him. "What did you say?" I target the torch directly at Sam's face. He shuffles backwards, eyes creasing from the light.

"I never told *you* Noah saw Dad with a map!" I straighten up. My voice as cold as the damp air.

Sam shields his eyes from the white light. "There's summat else I forgot to mention." He muffles a string of words. I catch "Noah" and "treasure" and "all my fault".

"How do you know Noah?" I cut across him, my

breath coming out in short, sharp bursts, when I jump – a violent banging noise from upstairs. Followed by the doorbell. Before – a bellow, loud and distinctive: "Open up! Police!"

# Thirteen

Small, shuffling steps in the hall above compete with my careless sprint up the shaky cellar staircase. Till I catch sight of Mum, greasy hair and grey skin arriving at the front door.

"No! Don't open it!" I hiss. I don't know what my fast heart fears more: the police outside or what they'll see inside. But I'm too late. Mum's pulling at the doorknob, like it's a giant boulder she's heaving away. Revealing them framed by a purple night sky.

The same Him and Her in black-and-blue uniforms from last time, four months ago, when they came about our broken boat. Standing the same way as last time: hats under their arms, expressions serious (Him) and worried (Her). "We're here about a reported missing person?"

Like last time, I hardly notice the quick flash of badges, the murmur of formal introductions: Detective Sergeant Something; Detective Constable Other. I hardly notice because I'm striding forward and I'm saying starkly on one breath, "Mybrotherisn'tmissing!" Because a sudden realisation is pinging in my head: Mrs Hollowbread! It'll be her who's gone "*reporting*"!

"Noah's just out exploring, finding." *Buried treasure.*

All eyes turn to me. Even Mum's black stones.

"Erm, yeah." I catch the arm-swinging bug from Sam and flush red. "We call it him going *Swallows and Amazons*, don't we, Mum?" I dart her a back-me-up glare.

"He'll be back for tea." I hurriedly speak for her, giving Him and Her in Blue my very best *yes-I-am-mature-for-thirteen* face. "Noah's favourite: eggs and beans," I fib.

"Our report doesn't mention any name. Just that someone's missing." Her in Blue cuts across me, her voice clipped and official. "We're duty-bound to follow it up," she says, before she lets out a worried gasp.

Because Mum's sinking on to the tiled floor like a wilting flower. "Oh, Faith, what have I done?"

"Mum?" My voice is suddenly as small as hers.

"I suggest we all have a cup of tea," Her in Blue clips to me, as if she already knows I'm Chief Teamaker. "Tea will see us right."

She turns to Mum. "You got a comfy sofa for us, Ms Walker?" And they start proceeding down the hall, *uninvited!* With Him in Blue staring into every nook and cranny, like he's taking police notes without a pencil.

I watch them disappear into the lounge and I sprint to the kitchen. "Oh yeah, tea will see us right," I mutter sarcastically under my breath. *Who needs TREASURE when you have TEA!* I give the cellar door daggers as I pass – I'm desperate to ask Sam down there, how come he knows so much about Noah, about our cellar! But right now, I've got to stop Mum from saying the wrong thing!

"We've no milk." I rush into the lounge with a lukewarm pot of tea because I couldn't wait for the kettle to boil. "Nor any sugar," I add, silently telling Her in Blue: *See! A cup of tea* isn't *going to see us right*.

I place the tray on the coffee table, my hands shaking so much the mugs rattle against one another. Him in Blue is standing by the window that looks on to the moonlit sea beyond, eyeing everything but the view. I brush the cellar dust and sticky cobwebs from my school trousers before he makes a mental note of that too. Her in Blue is on the scratched leather armchair; Mum's opposite on our tatty purple velvet, her eyes fixed on her lap. I drop on to the floor near her. She doesn't look well.

"So, let's get this straight." Her in Blue takes the longest inhale I've ever heard. "*Who* is missing here?" She directs the question to Mum, but I catch it, like I'm playing piggy in the middle.

"No one! Noah will be home in a jiffy!" I say in a voice

like the school nurse before she gives an injection.
(*I've never even used the word "jiffy" before!*)

Silence.

I notice Him in Blue has a notebook open now.

"I know who called you – Mrs Hollowbread," I pause
to think *the old bag*. "She's got it in for me."

Her in Blue frowns.

I shift position on the floor, willing Noah in my mind:
*See the police car; see we're in real trouble because
of your games. Noah, please!*

"Ms Walker." Her in Blue dips her head at Mum
like she's addressing a little child. "The call about a
missing person came from this house?"

I'm not sure how to describe the noise that leaks
out of my mouth, but it's loud enough and odd
enough for all eyes to turn on me again. My neck's
made of steel as I turn mine on Mum, picturing her
on the stairs earlier, phone in hand. *You brought the
police into our home?* I can almost hear The Lookout
groan around me.

"I didn't want to see," Mum finally speaks, fragile,
feathery; the police shift forward on their seats

to hear her. Him in Blue has found a pencil and is scribbling furiously in his little pad, tiny scratchy noises. The air grows prickly and the wind whistles through the gaps in the windows. The house ticks and creaks and clangs, demanding I *do something*!

"Tea anyone?" I ask brightly in my so-grown-up-for-thirteen best voice, and reach a shaky hand for the pot. "Noah's exploring, he'll be back ... in a jiffy." I start filling mugs with a milkless brew that I'm now desperately hoping *will* see us right.

"Ms Walker, if your daughter is correct about Noah," Him in Blue pauses pencil-scratching, "who did you report missing?"

More silence. The house ticks. The wind whistles. I keep pouring.

"Ms Walker?"

"I didn't call about Noah."

My breath seems to stop and pool in my lungs.

"Then who is missing, Ms Walker?"

I watch the tea overfill the mug and spill on to the tray.

Mum needs to go back to bed; stay quiet; *shush*!;

cup of tea; slice of buttered toast. Sleeping Beauty waiting for her Prince to return and kiss her back to being Old Mum.

A whimper behind me. "My husband."

"Dad's coming home," I murmur tightly, without taking my eyes off the teapot. The tray's a murky brown swimming pool.

Her in Blue's saying, "Your husband's not been seen for four months..." but Mum speaks over her, with wheezy, jagged breaths. "We had a row ... about the house ... I wanted ... us to leave."

There's a silent scream gathering momentum deep inside me, zigzagging through tunnels in my mind, barging through locked doors and leaping over high barriers. Louder than my "Dad" siren. Warning me: *Run!* Get away from Mum's fragile, feathery, voice before she can say something I can't hear. Don't want to hear. Except my body's become as heavy as our grandfather clock; my feet suddenly weighted like a stone anchor on the sea floor.

"I saw my husband, Ryan. I saw him go out in our boat."

The silent scream arrives, loud and fierce, right behind my eyes.

"He never came back."

*Crash.*

The teapot has slipped from my hand, smashing and splintering across the stone floor. Smashing and splintering like the pieces of Dad's boat they found.

I drop on to all fours, palms flat against the stone tiles. I can see The Crack outside, it's growing. It's going to split The Lookout in half!

"Ms Walker, are you now saying it *was* your husband who took out your boat, back in November?" Him in Blue.

I blink rapidly. Everything is going blurry; trembly; like there's an earthquake. *Is the ground shaking? Is the house moving? Are we slipping closer to the cliff edge?*

"You're not making sense, Ms Walker?" Her in Blue.

I turn to Mum. She's already staring at me, not through me; a liquid "sorry" filling her eyes.

"You said he'd upped and left?" My voice is hers; fragile, feathery. "You said he'd come back one day.

You said Dad left on foot. You said the boat was already on Redstone Beach; that the sea just claimed it. You said that."

*Liar!*

Mum told a fib worse than mine! A huge Burger King Whopper of a fib!

"Dad's gone?"

If you asked me what happened in the next few hours, I'd have to tell you that I can't be sure. Like a TV losing reception, my memories are fuzzy: snatches of colour and people and voices; time passing in a blur, coming and going, nothing is distinct. Everything is out of sequence.

Him in Blue scribbling more furiously in his pad, like he can't write fast enough. Her in Blue moving across to Mum and rubbing her back like she's a baby that needs winding and saying "just breathe" as if Mum's forgotten how.

I remember Him and Her whispering to each other in the hall. "Well, we all guessed he was lost at sea, didn't we?"

I hear them make calls, and I catch snatched words about boats and brothers and illness and intervention.

All the while, I seem to be looking down on myself from above: Old Me, Mean Me, Sad Me, Lonely Me – on all fours still, as if I'm escaping a shipwreck myself, scrabbling for pieces of broken teapot. *Find every piece! Get Dad's superglue! I can stick them back together!*

Do I remember locking the front door? I see Her in Blue, or was it Him, having to steer me away. "That's enough, Faith." Taking my key from me.

I see The Lookout's windows looming large, anxious stone-lintel eyebrows and sorrowful wood-framed eyes.

What next?

I remember Mum reaching for my hand in the police car. Or did I reach for hers? And it was cold. And I let it go again. *She lied to me.*

I remember their walkie-talkies buzzing and hissing with exchanged messages about a missing boy, red-haired, ten years old.

I remember sitting in the police station when

they decided Mum should go to hospital, for an "assessment" they called it, like she was going to take some exam. And Mum said nothing, just nodded, like she was a lamb needing herding. She replaced her *"can't"* with a constant trail of *"sorry"* to anyone who talked to her, but mostly to me.

I remember the stickiness of the green plastic seat in the station corridor. A nameless social worker quizzing me about Noah. About me. About Mum's BK Whopper of a lie. Using posh words about Mum like "trauma" and "denial". There was a pamphlet, she said. I didn't want another pamphlet. I wanted my dad.

He upped and left, Mum said. And I believed her. I *wanted* to believe her. And we carried on. Without him. And I fell out with Asha. And Mum took to her bed. And we avoided Other People. It was the only way I suppose ... not to fall off the edge.

# Fourteen

"Hello, Starling."

He's there. Lit up by the glow of a streetlamp through the thin curtains. Sitting all casual-like at the end of the bed: *What, me, dead?* Pulling that Joker grin he does on purpose to make me laugh. Except, he's not really here. And I'm not laughing. "I'm imagining you," I tell the fuzzy image, in case he doesn't know.

It's the first time I've pictured him properly, since he went. So I keep him there. I make him clearer. I paint in the deeper shade of his red hair, with the spray of silver in his sideburns. And I draw the creases at his eyes and the bracket lines round his wide frog-mouth. And I shift up in bed to whisper to him, "You've not called me Starling in ages."

"You never let me any more!" he says back. OK, I *make* him say back. "Not in front of your friends, not since you go to *big* school."

"And we don't call it *big* school!"

"*Uh, I'm so embarrassing!*" Dad's stroppy-teen voice; it used to, like, *really* annoy me. Now it makes my insides smile. Tease me as much as you like, Dad. *Just don't go.* But he can't hear that. And my eyes are heavy and straining to keep him projected there. He fades one bit at a time: lines, mouth, hair. I slump back heavily on to the pillow, and I stare into fuzzy-grey-nothing, and I wonder if The Crack isn't just in my garden, it's in me. Because that's how it feels. Like I'm splitting in half.

It's daylight when I wake again; it's over-hot and there's a strong smell of fake lavender. It takes my eyes a while to adjust, like when you come into the light after a dark cinema. I can still see Dad in my head, crinkly eyes, wide frog-mouth, but I don't picture him out of it again, not now I can see beyond the end of the bed. Dad doesn't belong among Aunty Val's flowery wallpaper and giant bowls of potpourri. He should be with the weathered gorse and yellow wallflowers that hug the coast. With the crash and soar of the sea, not the sound of car doors slamming and engines revving outside.

I perch up on my elbows and memories arrive like sea mist creeping veil-like over the fields. Bringing a recap, like you get at the start of a TV episode: Noah's still hiding somewhere. Mum's in hospital (she needs rest, they said. *When all she's done is sleep!*). And Dad. Dad's gone for good (my insides feel both heavy and empty at the same time).

"I'll miss my brother," I hear Uncle Art say in my recap, arriving at the police station to take me back to theirs, his voice as artificial as their lavender.

A sharp door-knock snaps me back to the present. Aunty Val sweeps in. "Oh, you're awake!" She looks disappointed. She flips opens the small bottle of anti-bacterial gel in her hands and squirts it over her palms.

"I'm not being funny, but you've been in bed, just lying there *for days!*"

"Days?" I sit up straighter.

"It's Monday! *Four.* Pee. Em! You've not eaten much."

I glance over at the bedside table – a mug of milky tea, a plate of curling toast. *Like Mum.* There's a sharp poke in my guts. "I need to get home." *Get us all back to The Lookout. That's what Dad would want!*

"Whoa there, hold your horses, missy. Your home wants featuring on ITV's *Houses from Hell* if you ask me!" She rubs gloopy palms together. "The police won't let my Arty near it! Some female officer with a weird name has your door key, she came over and brought you those." Aunty Val flicks a manicured hand at a neat pile of clothes on a chair; my rucksack below. "When I was all set to let you borrow what I've put out for the charity shop."

I silently thank Her in Blue.

"No, you're to stay here," Aunty Val gives an extra-long sigh. "While your mum sorts out her mental-what-not."

"Mum's going to be OK, isn't she?" My insides form a tighter knot.

"Post-traumatic-something or other, doc's saying." Aunty Val makes a face for *load-of-nonsense*, taps her forehead. "Meaning, it's all in there. She can't take care of you till they sort her meds out."

"But *I* take care of *Mum!*" And The Lookout! And... *Noah!*

"The whole town is out looking for the little fella." Aunty Val answers my next hurried question. "Police are keeping an eye on Hell House for when he comes back. They looked in that nasty cellar of yours like you told them. No sign of him."

"He's playing explorer," I say weakly. *But why hasn't he come back?*

"Hmm, well I always said to Art: 'Art,' I said, 'they give that small boy too much freedom!'" Aunty Val sniffs dismissively. "The landlord at The Ship Inn saw Noah snooping round his beer cellar with a torch Friday! Can you believe it, drinking at his young age!"

Another memory descends: Sam saw Noah on Friday too, with rope, at St Swithun's. *Sam!* I force my legs out of bed fast, my feet sinking into soft carpet not hard, creaky floorboards. *He knows something about Noah!*

"Any-hoo, what am I like! I almost forgot why I came up here: there're some visitors for you." Aunty Val pushes the door wider, bracelets on her wrist jangling as she beckons along the landing. "I've TV to catch-up on, so don't keep them here long, you hear?"

Then she adds, "Eat yesterday's toast, save me making more," before moving away to reveal the visitors: Asha and Sian, holding their shoes aloft.

They shuffle in. Asha's staring at the floor. Sian flicks critical eyes across the room, till they settle on me. "What *are* you wearing, Faith?" she says, as if nothing's changed; like it's just my old sassy mate Sian, come to my room in The Lookout to hang out and take daft selfies. "That's a serious fashion No Way."

I glance down: two Care Bears kissing – it must be a nightie from Aunty Val's charity bag.

I cross my arms tightly over my chest. Sian's expression shifts, as if she forgot too: we're no longer old mates who hang out taking selfies. "Sorry about your dad." She chews the corner of her mouth. "I liked him, he was good for a laugh, you know, but –" She looks around awkwardly. "Everyone said he was probably, like, drowned."

"Sian!" Asha bursts out, glaring across at her, before she *almost* meets my eyes. "Are you OK?" Hers look damp and shiny.

*Am I OK?* "I'm not sure," I say, sitting back on the bed and hugging my knees into the Care Bears. I don't know what else to say. I've not said much to anyone in so long. I should say sorry for blanking them. I want to say thank you for coming. But the last time I spoke to Asha and Sian I snarled at them, like one of those wildlife documentaries where a lioness is protecting her cubs. I was *so* angry; because they believed the gossip, about Dad and his boat and the sea. Gossip I couldn't listen to. Because it couldn't be true.

Aunty Val's Hoover starts up in the background.

"It's not fair –" Asha pauses, bundling her mouth together like she's trying not to cry – "that your dad's..."

"...dead," I finish for her. It's the first time I've used

that word out loud; it feels sharp and spiky on my tongue. It turns my bones stone-cold.

"Why did your mum tell you...?" Sian starts, but Asha must glare at her again because she shuts up.

"She – we – hoped he'd come back," I say plainly. I press my chin on to my knees and exhale hard through my nose.

"What's-not," Asha bursts out. Our secret code in primary school.

"What's-not," I repeat it this time, and I look up and she's staring straight at me. And I can see Old Asha in her serious brown eyes. And maybe she sees Old Faith in mine. And for a moment there my heart makes a little lift, like maybe life might slot back into place: Asha and Faith, BFFs since nursery, telling each other *everything*.

"Yeah, what-not, whatever the heck that means," Sian chips in. She tries smiling, even though smiling's never been her thing and adds, "Anyway, we're helping look for Noah." Digging into her coat pocket, she pulls out a piece of paper and passes it to me.

It's Noah, all freckles and school jumper, in black-

and-white. With "MISSING" written in bold at the top, and "Police Appeal" below. My skin prickles with fear. Despite what Aunty Val just said, his games suddenly seem *deadly* serious. *Oh, Noah.* I picture him: torch at the pub, rope at the churchyard – like he's playing some live game of Cluedo, except ... *wait* ... that map he drew, the map I binned! A felt-tip *steeple*, a pint of *beer*! St Swithun's and The Ship Inn! I scramble off the bed for my clothes, half-forgetting Sian and Asha are still there. "I've got to go," I turn awkwardly to them.

"Sure, OK. Mum's waiting outside anyway." Asha pulls the face she uses when she's trying not to look hurt. And I want to tell her *everything*, like we always used to. From the beginning. But I can't find the words to start that story either.

I imagine them looking at one another as they head downstairs; Sian looping fingers at her head; Asha mouthing, "Why won't she talk?" Maybe that's why my legs are tingling to run after them, tell them, *It's all right, I'm still here! Old Faith! You know, Faith who collects old postcards and gets freaked out by clowns!* I'll head out to the car with them for a warm "Faith, sweetheart!" from Dr Singh and she'll invite me back to theirs for dinner, like she always does. "Asha's dad will make his raita just for you!" she'll beam. That's after we've been for our post-school milkshake (candyfloss, extra whipped cream, sprinkles). And we'll watch daft cat videos and mess with selfie filters till we laugh so hard we're snorting cream out of our noses.

Like that's going to happen. Not when a Dad-sized chasm gapes between us.

"*Fix it!*" I hear Dad say on cue, sitting comfortably in my head like it's his new home.

I stare back at the Noah flyer on the flowery duvet. And start to speed-dress. First, I have to find my brother. Interrogate Sam, retrieve Noah's map! I grab my rucksack. *Help me bring Noah home,* I solemnly tell Dad back. *And I promise – I'll never lie again.*

I head downstairs in clean leggings and my mustard hoodie (thank you again, Her in Blue), with every last bit of change I could find at the bottom of my rucksack for the bus fare. Aunty Val has swapped hoovering for the phone in the kitchen. "I don't like having guests in my guest room," she's saying as I creep into the hallway, right as I spy Uncle Art's shiny briefcase on the hall table.

"Secrets and lies all surface in the end, Val," barks a familiar voice.

It's not the phone – it's my uncle she's talking to.

"I'm due a call from my mate at the council about The Lookout," he's continuing.

The words jolt me forward. In an angry flash, I flip the briefcase latches *click, click*, glimpsing it straightaway – the rusty tin box he stole from us – amongst Uncle Art's door keys, beard comb (eurgh) and a packet of humbugs. The box has a faded picture of a king – George the Third. Ancient. I open it gently. Inside, there's the old-looking envelope, with *"Father"* on the front; a small rusty key; and a tiny painting. I pick that out first – an oval-framed miniature of a girl. Side profile, dark lashes, determined expression, wild brown hair, in delicate watercolours. "Tess" is written on the back. "Hello, Tess," I whisper, before I swap it for the envelope. Her familiar hard-to-read writing is on the single page inside.

My dear Father,

I write in haste. I can hear survivors from Providence on Cliff Point! You must know the wreckers have sealed the tunnel to the cave, so the sailors have no chance of escape! Not while this storm rages on!

Father, I stood by as you allowed smugglers to dig their tunnels, even though they made vulnerable the ground beneath our home. I cannot stand by whilst you wreck a ship on purpose. God forgive you, Father, is our livelihood worth this?

I followed you - I removed the gold coins from your hiding place. Now, whilst you meet with your gang of wreckers to discuss how to sell what's not yours, I will hurry to save those whose lives you have destroyed.

I lift my eyes – Tess went to save the sailors. She died *with* them! – then lower them again.

*Father, the treasure is in time - until it can be reunited with its owners. If I do not return, I pray that your eyes will be opened to what you have done. You have turned our home into a house of greed and self-interest, and yet my heart remains full of love for you. We can-*

Her words end there. I hurriedly place everything back in the tin box. *The treasure is in time?* What does she mean? *Is that where you are, Noah?*

"Oi!"

I glance up sharply. Uncle Art's standing at the open kitchen door; shiny office-suit and a real cigarette, not his electronic one, lodged between two fingers. "What're you doing with that?"

"Stealing it back," I answer starkly. *I did just promise Dad not to lie any more.*

"It's mine!" He pushes out his hand for the tin box; his mouth scrunched up like a small child robbed of his favourite toy. "Listen, I'm very sorry about your father. But I did *my* grieving for Ryan when his smashed boat turned up months ago! I knew in here he'd gone!" His cigarette hand prods his gut, not his heart. "That you were making those phone calls up."

"Faith has one of those wonderful, vivid imaginations you often see in failing artists," Aunty Val chips in behind him, making a smile like it's a compliment.

"Now it's *my* turn as guardian of The Lookout." Uncle Art raises his two bearded chins.

"Then we can see what's hidden, isn't that right, Arty," Aunty Val interjects.

I glance between them. "You're just like the wreckers. You only want treasure. You don't care about finding Noah!"

Uncle Art's dark eyes dance. "Now you listen here! My brother kept secrets from me!" Voice rising; cigarette pointing. "Clearly wanted this so-called treasure to himself. I was right not to lend him money for that house!" His hairy chin fidgets furiously, as if he can't decide what he feels about that statement.

"Let's not make this unpleasant, Arty." Aunty Val looks appealingly at me. "My poor Arty didn't have a happy childhood. His mum and dad loved their house and his little brother more." Voice rising; painted-nail pointing. "He deserves compensating! Sent him back to tobacco, this has!"

She licks her lips. "Best place for you, young lady, is back to bed. Let me watch TV in peace." Forced smile. "You know, I could teach you how to do your hair, put a bit of mascara on those pale lashes. What do you think?"

*What do I think?* I furl my hands into tight fists. I hear Tess Walker's fighting words in her letter. I picture her determined expression in the miniature portrait. She sacrificed her life for strangers! I steel my eyes on Uncle Art's, like you stare down a gull who's after your ice cream – for once, I'm determined not to flinch. "I *THINK* I'm going to find my brother and take him *HOME*!"

It feels like a small victory when Uncle Art's the first to look away. Maybe that's what gives me the courage to grab his door keys from his briefcase. *Go!* Slam of the front door; I lock them both inside their over-hot, over-flowery, lace-twitching house.

"You get back here!" I hear Uncle Art shout as I run;
Aunty Val shriek, "Arty! What will people think!"

I know it won't take long for them to come round
the back or out a window, but luck must be on my
side for once. The number 44 appears just as I reach
the end of their cul-de-sac.

# Fifteen

Noah once pointed out where Mrs Hollowbread lives – one of those pastel-coloured terraced cottages on the riverside near Packhorse Bridge. Except, when I get to the river, I've forgotten just how many pastels there are. I'm resolving to knock on every one of them, pink, green, lilac, yellow – when I spot Noah in a porch window. Freckles; school jumper; "Missing" above his head; "Police Appeal" below. I ring Pastel Green's bell determinedly.

Mrs Hollowbread has a different

expression on her face than the one I'm expecting when she comes to the door. The moment she sees me, her prune mouth seems to flop and sag; her broad shoulders too.

"I'm so very sorry, Faith." She puts out a hand and holds it there, mid-air between us. "I hoped you were right, that your dad was coming back."

*Yeah, course you did.* I tuck my thumbs awkwardly under my rucksack straps.

"And your mother in hospital too..." Her face flushes like she's ashamed.

She should be! If she'd *never* made me lie about Dad coming back, I'd *never* have got mad with Noah and he'd *never* have run off!

"I'm staying with my uncle and aunt," I cut across the sympathy. "Who don't like guests in their guestroom."

If it wasn't for her, I could still be in The Lookout hoping Dad was going to come home! Something that's not my snake, more worm-like, squirms in my tummy, telling me that's probably stupid thinking. But still – "You shouldn't have interfered!"

I wait for her trademark snappish retort, for her prune mouth to reassemble, but she just becomes more flushed. She looks like she's about to say something else with "sorry" in the sentence.

"I'm only here to talk to Sam," I jump in.

"Samuel?" Her broad shoulders move back like she's been struck. "Why are you bringing up Samuel again? I don't understand."

"I know you want to keep him secret." My chest burns with a fury I want to keep firing at her. "So you can stay being mean to him!"

"Mean to him?" Her wrinkled eyes widen in alarm. "Oh, I was strict, far too strict, I know, but I-I've not seen him in so long." She breaks off, making a face like she's run out of breath. Before a noise that reminds me of Mum and grief comes out of her sagging mouth.

"I lost Samuel from my life fourteen years ago."

I'm half-running, half-stumbling down the path along the riverside. I could see Mrs Hollowbread was about to say more. No way was I going to stay to hear it! It's bad enough knowing: *fourteen years ago*?

When Sam's *my* age!

You've got to be kidding me.

She *lost* him? Lost as in ... *died*?

It suddenly all becomes clear, crystal clear – like one of Hercule Poirot's eureka moments, strong and shouty in my head:

1. Sam never changes his clothes and he stinks of the sea!

2. Sam likes that old band Oasis that Mum likes!

3. Sam said Noah told him about Dad's map!

I sprint faster over Packhorse Bridge, like I might outrun this new truth. But the facts present themselves so clearly, I have to halt abruptly again, as if the truth's standing there, solid as a wall in front of me:

*Sam is Noah's sea ghost!*

Only a ghost would appear magically in front of me without warning!

Only a ghost could find his way around our cellar without a torch!

Only a ghost would make a fashion No Way of

crocs'n'socks!

OK, so he's a modern-day ghost. Not a 1770 shipwrecked sailor. But it must be Sam Noah's been talking to! I shake my head – that *I've* been talking to. I've actually been talking to a *ghost*!

When just last week I didn't even *believe* in ghosts!

I continue to run, chewing on my thumbnail, trying to think as fast as my feet. Ghosts want things, that's what all the films and books say, that's why they stay on Earth. Well, that bit's easy: Sam wants the treasure that Tom Walker stole from *Providence*.

But why, if he's not actually from the shipwreck? I run quicker, chew harder, think faster. Noah said his sea ghost was protecting the others: is Sam some kind of ghostly detective? Or – maybe the Hollowbreads have an ancestor who's a *Providence* sailor? Like wrecker Tom Walker's mine? And ghost-Sam is seeking revenge on their behalf? A long, cold shiver surges through me. *I have to find Noah!*

I whizz through the churchyard and its lichen-stained gravestones. It's hard to believe I was here with Sam on Friday, talking to him like he's *human*!

Push on through the metal kissing-gate into the field; storming past pink Halfpenny Farm and the old well. Towards the brick pillbox and its head of grass hair, getting my first glimpse of The Lookout's stained slate roof. I tilt my head; something seems different. My tower roof looks slanted somehow, as if – *down*! I crouch sharply at the noise of Other People's voices; tops of heads turning off the road beyond. I wait till they're out of sight and pick up my pace; steel myself ready for Vicious Wind and Mean Wind and any of their other mates who want to try and stop me from finding my brother.

Except it's not any wind that halts me in my tracks.

"Faith!"

I jump, clutching a hand to my chest. Sam. The Ghost.

I turn slowly.

"I'm sorry about your dad, Faith," he says, joining me from behind the pillbox. His face looks grubbier (*can ghosts get dirtier?*), as well as sorry. Plus, he's missing one croc (*can ghosts lose shoes?*). His eyes look as damp and shiny as Asha's just did. (*Don't be stupid, ghosts can't cry!)*

"I heard your Mum telling the police from the cellar."
(*Nope: he already knew! Because he is a ghost!*)

I make a casual shrug back. I can't let him see my real feelings. I don't know how to play this yet. There's no pamphlet in the school library for handling vengeful ghosts.

"There was gossip about Dad, but I didn't want to believe it," I say in the blandest voice I can muster.

"Yeah, I know what that's like," Sam nods, biting his ghostly lower lip.

I pull a face at the unexpected ghost-empathy. "You do?"

"Course." Sam gazes round at the sea with a long sigh. Its waves are big and brown and frothy today. A lone seagull parades the shoreline like a soldier on duty. "I often pretend one day my real dad will come for me." He sniffs and rubs a finger under his nose (*can ghosts get colds?*). He glances over at my house. "Sometimes, I pretend I live there."

"*The Lookout*?" I say slowly. I take a gulp of a breath. Is he playing *pretend* now? Does he even *know* he's a ghost? There really should be a pamphlet for this in the school library. Except I've no time for ghost counselling. "In the cellar on Friday, what did you say about Noah?"

"I've been looking everywhere for him!" Sam's ghost-face seems to collapse a little. "All night!" (*Yep – because* ghosts *don't sleep!*)

"I didn't mean to..." he adds, before his voice trails off and he sneezes. I notice he's shivering too. If he wasn't already dead, I'd say he looked ill, the kind of ill Mum started to look.

"Didn't mean to ... what?"

"I'll find him, I will!" Sam says quickly, pushing his grubby hands through his dirty hair, so it stands to attention like Noah's does. "I'll help you!"

I shake my head. *Like I can trust a ghost! He's no better than Uncle Art; it's the treasure he wants to find, not my brother! And frankly, if he's not going to tell me where Noah is, I need to get on searching.* "I work better alone!" I turn and take fierce strides towards the house.

"But I've found some more stuff on 'wreckers' in

the library – it might help us!" Sam shouts after me. "It says they were ordinary smugglers who went rogue, that—"

"I don't want another history lesson!" I cut him dead (*literally*) and I sprint the last few metres on to my driveway. Rounding the garage, to the wheelie bin. I rip into the black bag, gagging from the sewer smell as I rummage past squidgy egg, sloppy cereal, stale uneaten toast. I wince as I prick my finger on the clock's broken glass, delving, until – *yes!* – I pull out the crumpled ball, flicking off clusters of Rice Krispies, ironing out soggy creases, and – Noah's map – my only clue to his exploring – is now a smudged, ink-leaked mess. The steeple and pint of beer are just blobs of felt-tip. All I can make out is a wavy line for the sea; possibly a cross beneath it.

Panic travels ice-hard from my stomach to my throat. I see Dad pulling our boat out from the garage, dragging it along the cliff edge. Noah wouldn't go out into the sea … would he?

I'm storming back to the driveway, leaving the bin's contents to the squawking seagulls circling me. I guessed he'd still be lurking there behind our hedge, in his stupid ghost-parka and his dirty ghost-croc (one), arms hanging limply by his side; looking like he's got nowhere to go but *here*; *my* home!

This time I don't hold back. "I know you've been haunting our cellar!" I hear my little brother's voice trying to tell me about his sea ghost. "I know it's you who sent Noah off on a stupid treasure hunt!" I shake the smudged, Krispie-soggy map at him.

"Tell me where my brother is!" I demand, placing my hands on my hips like Old Mum when she'd had it with me and Noah bickering.

Sam steps back, his own grubby hands spread out. "I don't know where Noah is, Faith," he says and he's either a great actor for a ghost or he's telling the truth.

My voice falters. "Have you got him locked up somewhere ... for *revenge* for what Tom Walker did?"

Sam the Ghost shakes his head frantically. "What you on about? I thought we were friends?" His voice sounds clogged (with *tears*? *Ghosts. Can't. Cry!*).

"I thought we were going to search for Noah and

the treasure together?" he says.

*Pretending! He said himself that's what he does!* I think of the smudged wavy line on Noah's map and the tide that will claim anything left on the beach, and my eyes grow bigger, threatening. "What've you done with my brother!"

Sam lets out a little yelping noise and bows his head.

I will *not* feel sorry for him. He's lying! London, Manchester ... he doesn't even know where he comes from!

Mean Wind seems to take its cue in the silence that follows, whistling and weaving round us, like it's goading us to fight.

"I didn't mean for him to run off!" Sam finally lifts his eyes. He seems to gulp back other words before he says, "I like Noah. I don't know anyone who gives owt for nowt!" He digs in his pockets and brings out his two ammonites.

"You said *you* found those," I bite back.

"I'm sorry." He dips his gaze again and lets out a ragged, watery breath (*pretending!*). "Noah said he was good at finding things."

"He is!" I should have listened to Noah. Then he'd be here. *Listened to Dad too*, and then maybe... Something throbs in the empty-heavy space where my snake used to live. *I never even said goodbye.*

I inhale, long and hard, filling my lungs with briny sea air. "What is it you want?" Even to my ears my voice sounds nasty, menacing. Maybe that's why Sam the Ghost raises his hands up in front of his face, as if I'm about to hit him.

"I want a home is all."

I hear the night-time screams. *Find home! Sam's* screams! "This is our home!" Gritted teeth. "Not yours!"

Sam steps away. "I only want what everyone's got ... warm bed. Food. I want to feel safe." He pulls his hands back down. A tear is slowly making its way down his cheek, forging a clear path through the dirt.

"W-well I just want my family," I throw back, unsure, suddenly, whether to make my voice steely (*Pretender!*) or soft (he does look really upset) – when we both catch the sound of Other People's voices.

"I can't get seen," Sam gasps. And with a magic puff he's gone, darting away; his retreating footsteps soon replaced by lots more. I peer round the end of our driveway. A large chattering gaggle, coming along Greystone Cliff. Parents with buggies; grey-hairs in sensible waterproofs; some teachers I recognise; Sheila with the tight perm from the Co-op. And at the very front – "Mr Kowalski!"

"Faith!" He breaks off from the group straight away, jogging towards me. His curly hair styled wildly by Vicious Wind and his friends. "It is wonderful to see you!" he says, and he looks like he means it. He lays a gentle hand on my shoulder. He doesn't need to add a "sorry, Faith," or pull a sympathy face. Behind his glasses, his eyes do all that for him. He digs into his trouser pocket and offers me one of his extra-strong mints. "We are all searching for Noah."

He points to the Other People walking past, and we stand there for a minute watching and sucking. Before I crack the mint in my mouth in two. I need hot breath to say it … the three words I've done my best to avoid. "I need help, Mr Kowalski."

I'm handing over Noah's soggy treasure map and digging out the ancient, rusty tin; Dad's book *Dorset Wreckers*. Finally, I need to tell someone the whole truth. Nothing but the truth.

I watch Mr Kowalski's kind eyes really listen, even if they skip and shine over the ghost parts. He listens so well I have to swallow a lump that's grown to the size and softness of a beach ball in my throat.

Other People. I suppose they're not so bad after all. It's like the fossil hunters on the beach. If you look hard amongst the rocks and chip away, you might find treasure.

# Sixteen

*We're not alone any more*, I tell Dad-in-my-head, as I stare hard at Noah's smudged map.

Mr Kowalski thinks the felt-tip steeple and pint of beer, along with the blocked-up tunnels in our cellar, mean Noah saw Dad with a map for smugglers – not treasure.

"Smugglers often used pub cellars and false gravestones as exits from their tunnels!" Mr Kowalski explained.

That's why he's gone this minute to take some searchers to St Swithun's and

The Ship Inn. I promised to join them soon, but first I need to try and think what the other smudges on Noah's map might mean. Try and put myself in my little brother's scruffy trainers.

"Live in a house like that?" Co-op's Sheila with the tight perm is leading a group of searchers past our driveway. "You'd have to be wild and daring," she's saying to someone.

I glance at my house. Its window-eyes reflect mine; they don't look wild or daring today. They shine with disappointment and despair.

"Wouldn't suit me," Sheila's voice becomes distant. "I get that lemming syndrome, you know – a mad urge to leap off any edge. I'd need to be tethered with rope to live –"

My heart makes a lemming-leap of its own. "That's it!" I gasp, as images collide in my head like atoms. I could almost run and hug Sheila with the tight perm. "Rope!" My eyes turn to saucers. Noah was carrying *rope*!

The darkening sky's looking stormy. Scraggy-looking, grumbling clouds congregating like there's some meteorological meeting above, as I sprint along the cliff path, breath panting, heart beating *bang bang bang*. Past the pillbox, Halfpenny Farm and its giant oak in the distance; straight towards a familiar sight I've never taken that much notice of – until now.

"Noah!" I begin shouting when I'm a few metres away. Because what else would my brother need rope for, except climbing down the old well? The cross between the church and The Lookout? It could be! My heart soars hopefully as I skid to a stop by the well wall and spy the metal mesh covering clipped and slashed open – and rope! Rope is tied securely to the old well bar!

"*No-ah!*" I scream with all my might into darkness, my hands gripping the top of the rough stone wall. Wishing I could shut up those machine-gun gulls; the roar of the waves; grumbling clouds; silence the whole world, so I can hear –

Nothing. My heart thumps to the bottom of my stomach. *What if he's there, but badly hurt?* I reach for my phone, my guts twisting into multiple tight knots, when –

"Fay?" Faint, but –

"*Noah!*" My skin tingles with relief. "Are you OK?" I peer into nothingness till my eyes make out, *yes*, a small, shadowy shape! Fast, I press 999 for the first time in my life. "I'm getting help!"

I glance back at my phone. *No signal!* I dart across the field: *still none!* I'm thinking of running to the church for Mr Kowalski, when a groan rises up louder from below. "Faaay! Don't…!"

I rush straight back, my hands instinctively reaching for the rope, tugging it to check the knot is secure, like Dad taught us to on boats. "I won't leave you! I'm coming, Noah!" I say, thinking fast in my head of a plan: get down, check he's OK; climb back up and run for Mr Kowalski. I clamber up on to the wall, squeezing myself between the torn metal mesh, wincing as the sharp edges snag and tear my leggings, scratching my skin beneath.

*No different to abseiling at Year Six residential,* I try and reassure myself as I edge my way down, my feet flat against the well wall, a strong smell of stagnant water filling my nostrils; Noah calling out faint words

I can't hear above the beating of my heart. I keep Tess Walker's determined, painted profile in my head, going out to sea to save the sailors of *Providence*. I'm just going down a well to save one brother! It helps me push faster with my feet, to ignore the searing palm burns from scaling the rope. Down, down.

"*Aaaargh!*"

The rope ends before I feel floor beneath my feet. I fly what must be a good few metres, elbows and hands meeting hard stone as I land with a violent bump; a painful twist of my ankle.

I hear Noah's voice close to my ear, scratchy and weak, with a familiar tinge of brotherly annoyance. "Said *don't* ... rope too short."

I scramble up, drinking him in like my brother's water in the desert. Red hair dark with grease, freckles mingling with dirt; I'd forgotten how his eyes are like Dad's. My heart seems to spill over.

"Aw, Noah!" My bruised arms hug him tightly, as he winces, and he groans.

"Why do you never listen, Faith..."

# Seventeen

Nope, my brother's right (again) – I can't reach the end of the rope no matter how high I jump (which isn't far with a sprained ankle). I think Noah might have broken his arm. Though the explorer in him probably saved his life – he packed food, water, and a sleeping bag in his overnight explorer bag.

There's zero chance my phone will get a signal down here, and my voice is now as hoarse as Noah's from shouting for help. The meeting of grumbling clouds above soon reaches a resolution and rain drives down the well. No one will hear us above that.

"Don't worry." I tuck myself around Noah to protect him from the worst of the rain and I try and sound reassuring. "Mr Kowalski will be searching here next, I'm sure."

"You'll like Mr Kowalski," I add, because talking distracts me from worrying. "He said, once we find you, he'll sort emergency funding for The Lookout." I think again of the lean to my tower room. "He knows about old houses and history."

"Does he know about ghosts?" Noah says, in his scratchy old-man voice.

"He does now," I reply gingerly. "I told him." Even in the greying light I can see Noah's face flooding with *told-you-so*.

"Sorry." I make a sound of defeat. "I spoke to your sea ghost, Sam – northern accent?"

"Yeah, s'pose. He never told me his name."

"Grubby looking, wears crocs, right?"

"I never saw him either, I told you. Crocs?"

"Yeah, he's a recent ghost. He lied to you, he's not

from the shipwrecked *Providence*. He likes crusty museums and old pop bands and has a dimple in his left cheek." I picture Sam's crooked-teeth smile and a pleasant feeling swirls in my stomach. "He wants our home. We can't trust him," I clip, annoyed at myself for almost forgetting – *he's the enemy!* "I bet he knows you were trapped down here!"

"You're wrong!" Noah grimaces and clutches his hurt arm as he straightens up. "He's my friend. He *is!*"

I make a murmuring noise like Old Mum did when she agreed just to shut us up. Tell him to rest his arm; that, *fine*, we'll visit sea-ghost Sam once we're out of here and uncover the truth about him once and for all. "You and me together." But first, he'll have to hear about Dad. I move back into human umbrella position. I just hope Mum is getting well enough to do that for me.

The rain is easing, but the circle of sky at the top of the well is turning from dirty purple to black. Hundreds of pinprick stars are appearing now the sun's switched its light off. I try and wish on the brightest. That someone will save us soon.

Before Noah's arm gets gangrene, or we both starve. Or the "other" ghosts appear. That last one makes me send up one long, last cry of "Help!"

For a moment there, I think I hear another voice travel back through the air. Vicious Wind, up to its usual tricks? I strain my ears for ages to hear it again, past the drip-drip of water in the well; the crash and hiss of waves; the clouds taking their grumbles further down the coast; a siren.

A siren?

I squeeze Noah's good arm. *It is!* "A siren!"

It keeps getting closer.

Brakes screech; doors slam; voices holler.

A shadowy face in luminous green appears above, framed by stars.

"I'm Sally. I'm a paramedic," Luminous Green says. She might as well be Father Christmas, I'm that excited to see her.

I watch the fireman ("Toby") take Noah up first, cradling him in a swing seat. By the time I'm brought up, they've got him wrapped in silver foil like a marathon runner while Sally the paramedic shines a light into his eyes at the back of an ambulance; that's next to a fire engine; that's next to a police car. My insides shrink at all this attention, when I've tried so hard for so long for no one to notice us. Now I have every force out.

"We should've thought to check places like this," says a familiar voice behind me. Her in Blue. She looks less efficient, more frazzled, as she takes over from Toby and leads me towards the ambulance. "Thank goodness your mate called."

"My mate?"

"Yeah, the lad who called us?" she says. "He knew both your names. He sounded really cut up."

*Sam?* A wobbly voice in my head answers. *Ghosts don't phone!* I silently shout back, like I'm in a pantomime, as Her in Blue asks another paramedic ("Bill") to check me over.

"I'm really impressed with you, Faith," she says when Bill's finished. She gives me a friendly wink. "Here, I won't be needing this any more." My house key. "For when you go home." Another wink.

"They'll get you a warm cup of tea at the hospital,"

she adds with a wave. Because, clearly, she still believes tea will see everything right.

I only remember at the last minute to call after her. "What's your name?"

"DS Strangler," she shouts back, with a grin that says, *I know, what a name.*

I really don't know how I missed it before.

Noah becomes more Noah-like in the ambulance, now his arm is all trussed up and he's using an oxygen mask that's making him act like he's eaten all the chocolate Hobnobs. He won't stop questioning Sally the paramedic on everything he sees: "What's that machine for?" and "Is that to restart hearts?" and "Can I press that button?" I reckon Sally and Bill are pretty relieved by the time we reach Exeter hospital and Noah's wheeled away.

A nurse called Makayla with massive pink-rimmed glasses and tiny black braids takes charge of me, bandaging my sprained ankle in a cubicle with a curtain round it. She's clearly read *1000 Jokes To Make You Laugh* as she keeps trying lots out on me, to stop me worrying about Noah. When she gets me that cup of tea (and a whole plate of biscuits), she also brings news at last: "A fractured humerus, torn ligament in his foot, a little dehydrated, maybe some shock." She pauses to smile. "But he's going to be fine." I'm not sure why she didn't start with the last one, but I forgive her because she has the best glasses and the worst jokes, and she says next, "Let me take you to see him."

I don't recognise her at first, the woman with clean, brushed hair, sitting in a dressing gown beside Noah's bed. Whose eyes when she turns round are no longer black stones and bloodshot; they're green and wide; the kind that can hold mini-stories.

"Oh, Faith," Mum says, her whole face collapsing into one big *sorry*. And suddenly I don't care that she lied about Dad; I'm just so glad to have my family back.

We've not had a group bundle in a long time. When all four of us would tumble into one another till you could hardly breathe and you didn't know whose arms were whose. Probably not since I started secondary school; since I said I was too *old* for them. But a group bundle now, even without Dad, feels like the best thing in the world. When we finally pull apart, Noah shifts in his bed and the metal frame makes a noise like a massive fart. And Noah says, "It wasn't me!" And tries and fails to prove it, which makes me burst out laughing for the first time in an age, and that starts Noah laughing too, and before long it starts Mum laughing as well, like some laughter relay race. And I keep laughing even though the bed-frame fart isn't really *that* funny, just to keep Mum laughing, because the sound of it – it's almost like Old Mum is back. Almost.

Nurse Makayla lets us stay together all day. "Even when visiting time's over," she whispers. I try not to think again about Sam (he's welcome to the treasure for all I care) and whether ghosts can use phones and lose crocs and cry real tears. I don't want to think about anything else, not even about my house (I'll leave it to Mr Kowalski to do the saving now).

I watch Noah scoff triple-helpings of Cheerios ("your favourite again?") and Mum actually eat (not eggs and beans). And I feel helpless while Mum holds

Noah and tells him about Dad. And I try not to focus on the tightening in my tummy when Noah says that, actually, he'd wondered about it already. "Sam the sea ghost told me dads don't usually come back."

And we both listen while Mum finally explains, in a voice that's no longer quite as fragile and feathery, how Dad "became obsessed with some tin box he discovered in the cellar".

"I tuned out; stopped listening," Mum said; her eyes filling with tears. She didn't know about the blocked-up smugglers' tunnels till the night he left. "Your dad showed me this map, with a cross for where the smugglers' tunnel began – the cave at Cliff Point. He was convinced he'd find gold coins there!"

She wished she'd not shouted at him, she said. She never imagined he'd take the boat out in a storm, just to prove he was right. "Till I saw him from the bedroom window. It was too late to get him to come back."

A sea fog crawled into her mind, she said, dense and blinding; burying her thoughts. She just wanted to hide, to sleep, until everything magically went away.

By early evening, Noah starts to fall asleep and another nurse ("Iris": brisk eyes, no jokes) takes over Makayla's shift and insists "visiting time *is* over" and Mum "needs her rest". They can't find me a bed at the hospital, Nurse Iris says, marching me into the corridor; she wants to call Uncle Art because he's listed as my temporary guardian. And I'm trying to find a way to explain why I can't go back to their flowery guestroom that's not for guests.

"They're your family." Nurse Iris looks peeved with me.

"They're not," I say back. Because it's the truth. Asha and Sian were family. Mr Kowalski is more like family. Even DS Strangler, Sally and Bill the paramedics, Makayla with the massive pink-rimmed glasses, have acted more like family.

Nurse Iris's peeved face gets more peeved. "Who else will you stay with if not your uncle?" Her voice has a new edge of exhaustion.

I'm thinking whether I'm brave enough to ring the Singhs, when a voice behind says, "She can come home with me."

I glance round, confused, thinking it's another nurse, because the voice sounds soft, kind. But it's not a nurse. "Mrs Hollowbread?" I'm not sure whether to say or spit her name.

She moves closer, holding her coat over one arm, patting it like she's nervous. Her prune lips fidget, struggling with a smile. An *actual* smile.

"I came as soon as I heard the news about Noah," she's saying, *softly, kindly*. "But I didn't want to disturb you all. So, I've just been waiting." She gestures with her patting hand, as if to say, *and here I am*. Clears her throat. "I still feel responsible."

*So you should.*

"If your mum agrees, I have a spare room."

What's that expression? Out of the frying pan into the fire? I've never properly understood it before. Well, I do now! From Uncle Art's wolf's lair to Mrs Hollowbread's witch's hovel? *No, thanks!* I'm turning back to Nurse Iris, ready to recite Asha's home number, when Mrs Hollowbread pushes a hand out. She touches my arm gently, cautiously, like I'm the stern adult and she's the nervous child.

"Faith, we never got the chance to talk about Samuel. You could tell me how you know him. I think it upsets me more than I realise. He's hardly been in touch all these years, you see."

I sense my jaw drop open. *Hardly ... in touch?*

There's an impatient sigh from Nurse Iris behind.

"But I thought you *lost* Sam?" I make a hard swallow, "As in '*died*' lost?"

Mrs Hollowbread's jaw mimics mine. "Died?" She looks stuck for words. "I've not seen Samuel since he left home at eighteen. I get the occasional postcard every few years."

"He left home at *eighteen*?" Sam the ghost is no way eighteen. "*Alive?*"

"That's right." Mrs Hollowbread looks more confused.

"Shall I call your uncle?" chimes peeved-exhausted Nurse Iris.

I make a snap decision. "Yes, if it's OK, Mrs Hollowbread. I'll stay the night with you."

I really don't expect the broad smile I get in return. A smile that might not hold crooked teeth but makes a dimple in her left cheek and instantly reminds me of someone else I know, with eyes just her shade of blue.

# Eighteen

Her little cream Mini still smells of petrol and pine. But apart from that, nothing else seems the same. Mrs Hollowbread's sloping shoulders suddenly don't look so broad, her hair bun not as severe; her whole face appears – more human. I'm not sure if she's changed, or if it's the way I'm looking at her. Maybe it's both.

"He said you were his gran." I'm still trying to explain. "The Sam I know."

"His gran?" The car wobbles a bit on the dark country road, before sensible Mrs Hollowbread comes to a not-so sensible abrupt halt. "There was a strange boy at my house the other day!" She lets out a little gasp. "I shut the door on him. I thought he was trying to sell me fossils!"

"Sam," I say. "He wanted to give you an ammonite, to pay you to take care of him. *Might* he be your grandson?"

Another gasp. "I dismissed it as idle town gossip back then; I had far worse concerns about my son's behaviour to contend with." She clamps a hand to her broad chest. "That old rumour that Samuel got some girl pregnant?" She glances sharply at me. "Is your Sam my *Samuel's* child?"

A car beeps then screeches round us, the driver doing rude things with his fingers as he passes. I touch Mrs Hollowbread's arm and gently suggest we keep driving.

By the time we've reached town and she's parking the car at the back of her terrace, I've told her everything I know about Sam. Which I've got to admit, I'm ashamed is almost nothing. I never asked him about his mum, or about his mum's horrid boyfriend.

I never asked why Sam had no money for a bus fare. I didn't even look at his favourite museum display, the Victorian pharmacy.

"Enough talk – bed, young lady!" Mrs Hollowbread insists loudly, as she cuts the engine. And I have to admit I'm starting to feel as drowsy as Mum looked. I let Mrs Hollowbread steer me down a narrow path and through a back door, like I'm little again, and getting carried in by Mum or Dad after a long, night-time journey. I briefly inhale another-house-smell, before I'm guided up a narrow staircase that creaks satisfyingly; handed a large T-shirt (no Care Bears) and a spare toothbrush. The moment my head hits the pillow, I must fall asleep, because I don't remember much else.

Mrs Hollowbread's house is a home. That's what I think first when I open my eyes. Another guest room – except this time, there's a mish-mash of old furniture, ornaments (mostly frogs), and no flowery wallpaper. I can hear ducks outside, and the water slopping against the sides of the riverbank. A kinder sort of wind rustles trees nearby. Dad would like it here.

I get up, reaching for yesterday's clothes. They smell musty and my leggings are ripped like I've been in a cat fight; there's all kinds of dark stains on my mustard hoodie. It instantly makes me think of Sam and his dirty parka; real and human ... and clearly *living* in our dark, damp cellar. It wasn't Noah raiding our fridge and cupboards. The thought scratches at my throat, as I quickly finger-comb my hair, a face-splash in the bathroom, and head down the narrow creaking staircase (more ornaments – she *really* likes frogs) towards the breakfast smells.

"Oh, you can wear your shoes inside," Mrs Hollowbread says as I enter the snug kitchen at the back of the house, carrying my trainers. She's at the hob wearing an apron with "Star Baker: Genevieve" on it, and there are two cats, one brown, one ginger, stretched out on the window sill overlooking a garden that's wild and cosy at the same time. Really – if you'd asked me to draw the house Mrs Hollowbread lives in, well, it wouldn't have looked anything like this. But this new version of Mrs Hollowbread suits it perfectly. Which makes me wonder again, if I ever had her right in the first place.

"Bonnie and Clyde," Mrs Hollowbread says, when I go over to stroke the cats. "That's it, they like a fuss being made of them." She laughs. "Don't we all." Then she pauses mid-bread slice and gives me one of those looks that adults make before they're about to say something serious. I push my fingers deeper into ginger fur and brace myself.

"I've acted wrongly, Faith. I was concerned for Noah, but I should have tried talking to you. Properly. You'd think I'd have learnt. After making the same mistake with my own son, Samuel." She pats lips together that no longer seem prune-like, just lived-in and regretful. "Moving back here last year – I thought I could put the past behind me." She shakes her head sorrowfully. "Instead, it only reminds of how I lost my son; makes me angrier at myself." She sighs. "At others."

"Your son still might come home one day," I say hopefully.

Mrs Hollowbread makes a face like she thinks that's unlikely. She waves her bread-knife. "You know, I see the parents lining up to collect the pupils and often they look more unsure and anxious than their children." She makes a little laugh, the kind when nothing's funny. "I fear we humans accumulate more questions than answers. Like a snowball." She puffs out her wrinkled cheeks, to make me laugh, like Nurse Makayla yesterday. I do, the kind of laugh when something *is* funny. I sort of like hearing my own laugh again.

"Now sit and eat!" Mrs Hollowbread becomes teacher again. She won't let me lift a finger, not even when I tell her I'm a professional tea and toast maker. Maybe that's why I'm suddenly famished – like really famished – because someone else is cooking for me again. I wolf down three warm croissants; smear big lumps of "my friend Pat's homemade strawberry jam" on to toast; gulp back freshly squeezed orange juice. Till I remember Sam. How lonely and hungry he must be. If I think about it, I do know more about him.

"*My* Sam – I think he's mad about history," I tell Mrs

Hollowbread. "He likes museums with no buttons, and he's got this infectious laugh and he can get excited really quickly." I pause and press my lips together. "I think his mum's got a mean boyfriend. I think maybe he's run away from home."

Mrs Hollowbread lets out a noise that starts with "oh" and ends with "argh", before she frowns and says, "I have a grandson," in a way like she's playing with the sound of the words.

I'd tell her where he might be. Except I also know it must've been Sam knocking over our clock, when Mrs Hollowbread visited. That Sam likes the museum empty and the library crowded. He's trying to stay hidden. I know how that feels.

"This is what we'll do: you'll rest for now, Faith." Mrs Hollowbread lifts a silencing hand when I start to protest. "I'll take you to see your mother when I'm back from school." She smacks determined lips together. "I'll make some calls, go through the proper channels to track down Sam's mother. Find out where his home is."

*Home.* I feel a punch in my stomach as I hear Sam

telling me, "*I want a home is all.*" I push my plate away. My appetite's gone.

*Sam* – I practise my speech to him in my head, as I hobble with a sprained ankle and two croissants stuffed in my coat pockets through the field towards home. Well, Mrs Hollowbread never said "resting" wasn't a bracing coastal stroll, did she?

Sunshine is making the world look bright, hopeful; the first colours of spring are sprouting through the hedgerows and the sky is a clean sheet of blue paper. Mind you, the Halfpenny Farm cows are all crowding under the giant oak like they know something the weather reporters don't.

I'm trying my very best not to think of Sam having left already. Never seeing Sam again makes my empty insides even heavier. It makes me miss Dad more. It makes me feel sorrier for Mrs Hollowbread and her lost son – Sam's father – who won't talk to her.

I pass the well, where there are people in council uniforms sealing it up with metal and hammers. "Sam," I practise, "your gran's not fairy-tale mean after all! Two cats, one brown, one ginger; lots of (v. odd) frog ornaments; oh, and I think her name's 'Genevieve'. I *know*, Genevieve! And *ahhhh* – there's such a homely smell to her house, Sam!"

On past the pillbox, the grey-blue of the sea and The Lookout in my sights. There's something still not quite right about my house: my tower room really does look like it's tipping forward; in fact, is the whole house leaning? I rub at my eyes, watery from the salty wind, and get my key out. It's just an ancient house that's lived many years; bending like a tired, old woman.

"Sam?" I peer into the cellar darkness, phone torch out. The musty, damp smell beats fake lavender any day. "I've got breakfast for you!"

No answer; except from The Lookout: creaks, clicks, sighs. The voices of all the people who have lived and loved here, Dad said. Maybe that's why I can suddenly hear laughter and shouts; kitchen chats and door slams; "no balls inside"; "dinnertime!"; Friday-night-film-night blaring. *My family*; we're in the house's past too. We're part of its shadows and empty spaces.

The thought makes me want to find Sam even more badly. I take the cellar stairs quickly, wishing I'd eaten more carrots. It's empty. Into the coal bunker. Empty.

"Sam!" I shine light on the cabinet there, a thought striking in my head like a match. *What if?* I heave it away, move on to hands and knees, through the hole, into the right tunnel, away from the noises of the sea. *What if this is how Sam came and went without being seen?* The tunnel's so thin I have to almost slide on my stomach, like a worm through soil. My rucksack scrapes the ceiling; my palms and elbows, still sore from falling down the well, soon sting and burn. I'm really regretting eating all those croissants now, starting to get panicky – when my phone lights up rough stone wall ahead: *a dead end*, like Sam said.

I let out a moan and try turning round in the thin space, pushing on the tunnel ceiling for leverage, jolting back as it moves. *It's falling in!* A scuffling noise above. I pause, push again at the ceiling. A shaft of light – it's a trapdoor. I push my head up through it, catching sight of his grubby face before he scuttles away like a hermit crab.

"Sam! Wait!" I shout after him.

He's gone by the time I clumsily hoist myself out, adjusting my eyes to gloomy daylight. I realise in an instant where I am: the Second World War pillbox. That Dad told us never to enter. Soon after he banned us from the cellar! I think of Sam popping up, *always* near the pillbox. The smugglers' cross on the map! *Not* the well, like Noah guessed!

He's somehow made it into a "home": a cardboard box for a table; a piece of string for a washing line, strung with – *oh, underpants*. I quickly look away again. There's that sleeping bag I saw last in the cellar. A battered teddy face pokes out the top. It looks as grubby as Sam. Nearby, there's a pile of familiar food wrappers. *There went the chocolate Hobnobs!*

Recognising Noah's well-thumbed *Swallows and Amazons* on the cardboard-box table, I pick it up; the bookmark's a folded report – from a school in Manchester. He did lie about London then. "*Seth Samuel Hollowbread*". His first name's Seth? He must be proud of the report to bring it with him. I don't blame him, even if all his teachers report he doesn't say a lot, some of his grades are amazing – especially history. It's only as I'm placing it back down that I spot Tom Walker's old brass telescope. Noah must have given it to him along with those fossils. I grab it and duck out of the doorway, shouting for him again, "Sam! Seth!"

I head past Cliff Point, towards Greystone Beach, because that seems to be his favourite, like Noah. Fast along the cliff path, ignoring the sharp stabs of pain in my sprained ankle. I stop to search through the telescope... A distant dog-walker ... a discarded lobster basket...

I wish hard that I'll find him, just like I wished hard for The Crack to disappear that morning when I first found Sam on the beach. Maybe it's magic after all.

...two seagulls fighting over a fish carcass ... a blue parka. My stomach fizzes, skips – *Sam!* A huge grin on my face, I run limping. For once Vicious Wind is on my side, acting like a sail behind me, propelling me forward so I'm almost flying, and I start to recognise the fizz and skip in my stomach – I'm excited to get my friend back.

Down the steps to the beach, ready with my practised speech about the "home" waiting for him with Mrs Hollowbread, who is more fairy godmother than wicked witch. Who makes a mean breakfast; clearly has a weird obsession with frogs; has cats, one brown, one ginger; has eyes his shade of blue. Except he doesn't look up as I call his name; he purposely looks away. I can imagine the scowl chasing across his face.

Maybe that's why I hear my voice – loud and encouraging – across the wind: "I think I know where the treasure is, Sam!"

# Nineteen

"Err, our blow-up dinghy." I point despairingly at the half-deflated blue and yellow boat in the garage, that Noah and I use in the sea when the water's calm and warm. *Not* in early March when grumbling clouds collaborate and the sea's as cold as ice. This is such a bad idea. I don't know why I said that about the treasure. I just wanted him to like me again. I glance at Sam (first name Seth). He's not said a lot since Greystone Beach; he only shrugged and pursed his mouth when I told him about Mrs Hollowbread.

Only a quiet, "Let's go then," when I explained what Mum said, that Dad believed the gold coins to be at Cliff Point cave.

I admit, I'd imagined a more enthusiastic reunion.

"The thing is –" I turn to him now, remembering how he made me say sorry at the bus station before he'd talk to me. I arrange my face into *truly, deeply* apologetic. "– I was a bit mean to you."

"A *bit*?" He flashes me a look, then stares down at his crocs. I see he's wearing both again. Though his socks look dirtier and damper than usual. He still looks ill – his nose is running and his lips are more chapped than ever.

"Erm, see, I kind of thought you were a ghost, seeking revenge."

Sam's eyebrows twitch. "Oh." Something shifts across his face. "Oh," he says again. "Yeah … hmm, I sort of pretended—"

"I know everything already," I break in carefully.

"I didn't mean to get him hurt," Sam's voice rises like I'm accusing him. The toe of one croc circles the garage floor. "I needed somewhere to sleep, and your front door was open one day."

I roll my eyes. "*Noah.*"

"I hid in your cellar and found the tunnel to the pillbox..." His shoulders slump. "I'd nowhere else to go. Not till I could work out how to get my gran to take me in."

I'm about to launch in about Mrs Hollowbread again, that the only thing wicked about her is her breakfasts, when Sam stretches his mouth into a determined line. "Then Noah heard me. Couldn't have him telling on me, could I? Get me sent back up to Mum's." He makes a small shiver and shoves both hands into his parka pockets. "Only meant to scare him off with my shipwrecked ghost story. Instead he kept coming down to talk to me!" Sam gives a little laugh, before he fixes me with serious eyes. "When I told him about the *Providence* gold coins, your brother said he was good at finding things. Said he'd seen his dad with a map with crosses." His eyes move wildly. "I never knew he'd go off down a well, did I!" He pauses. "I could've really hurt him. All cos I pretended to be a ghost!" He makes a sheepish face. "I used to love drama at school."

"Me too," I say, to show him again I don't blame him. "Houdini as well?" I try a joke. "I mean, how *did* you get out of the cellar door once I'd locked it?"

Sam takes a long breath. "You learn quick how to unlock doors when your mum's boyfriend likes to shut you out the house."

"Is that why you scream at night?" I say quietly.

He rubs his cheek like he's embarrassed. "I took my sleeping bag into the cellar when it was raining. Mum's boyfriend thrashes me for screaming in my sleep."

"Thrashes you?"

Sam frowns so hard the lines on his forehead turn pink. "He says I cost him too much to feed."

We both go quiet and stare at our feet. "You know, Mrs Hollowbread really does want to meet you." I look up at him again.

"Yeah, right. Won't want me living with her though, will she?"

"Course she will," I say, though now I think about it, I can't remember her saying those exact words. In fact, she mostly talked about proper channels and finding Sam's mum.

"No one does owt for nowt," Sam mumbles, as if he can read my mind. His eyes brighten just a little. "If we find gold – maybe I could pay for some boarding school to take me in. I like school."

I glance at him strangely. Before I start collecting oars and beach towels and life jackets. Sam needs the gold coins as much as The Lookout. I suppose we're going on a treasure hunt after all.

Sam's arms have a little jig to them again, as he takes the front end of our newly pumped-up blue and yellow dinghy along the cliff path towards Redstone Beach steps. *See, right decision*, I tell myself, even though my feet are turning to concrete in my trainers. We pass the council sign that warns: *No swimming near cliffs at peril of death* with a drawing of a swimmer crossed out in red. I try not to picture Dad.

By the time we're making slow progress across wet, heavy shingle, I've filled Sam in on the rest of Tess Walker's letter and her heroic bid to save the stranded sailors. "Dad must have guessed Tess took the treasure with her. Before she drowned with all the sailors," I add sadly. I look at the waves lapping the shore. *Don't picture Dad.*

"Tess must've been dead brave," Sam chirps back.

"So are you," I say in earnest. "Escaping your mum's evil boyfriend."

There's a blush spreading beneath the dirt on his cheeks as he glances round. "Maybe we can donate some of the gold to a lifeboat charity."

"Good idea," I say quietly. *Don't picture Dad.*

"I've never won owt in my life!" Sam pipes up excitedly as we drop the dinghy by the side of the cliff. "Not even on the penny-drops at the arcades!" He makes his crooked-mouth smile. And I try and smile back, even though the concrete in my trainers is getting denser now we're at the water. I remind myself we're both wearing life jackets. (*Dad never took his!*) And the sky's still a sheet of paper blue. (*Not like the storm Dad sailed in!*)

We take off shoes/crocs, roll up leggings/trackie bottoms, and leave our stuff under a rock overhang that juts out like a shopkeeper's awning. Before dragging the boat into the shallows, sucking in our breath with an "aargh" and an "urghh" at the same time as the icy chill takes bites at our legs. I hear Dad warning me and Noah: "*You die of cold before you drown.*" For some reason it gives me a rush of hot anger.

I steady the boat and order Sam to jump in, before I follow, quickly grabbing the oars before the waves push us back to shore. Strong strokes, to steer us towards the cave at the end of Cliff Point that's shaped like a human face (OK, *Noah*, a horse's head.) The sea's calm enough to glimpse the lion's paw that stretches out from it; a long line of dangerous, jagged rocks beneath the surface of the water, waiting to snare ships and snag swimmers. Out here, it suddenly becomes too easy to imagine a ghost ship, a galleon with tall cream-coloured sails, like the model in the museum, battling waves in a storm. I glance back towards land – I can almost see the glow of Tom Walker's lantern lit far away, leading *Providence* to think the danger was further down the coast, until –

*Crash!* My insides turn to concrete like my feet.

The waves are getting higher as we get deeper. The sea sprays us with water; salt stings my eyes. I make longer, stronger strokes with my left oar as we get closer to the cliff end. Another shower of sea on to the boat, like the waves want my attention. To show me more of their stories. *Don't picture Dad.* A strange anger's growing, like a wave inside me too. *I can't stop it* – I see Dad. Sailing in our wooden boat with his map, set on saving The Lookout; proving a point to Mum. As foolish as Tom Walker! Tom Walker, who helped wreck *Providence*!

A painful fury stabs the middle of my chest. *Dad* wrecked *our home!*

"My ancestor, Tess Walker, went to save people," I shout aloud at Sam. "We're just risking our lives for greed; like smugglers!"

Sam looks round at me. "Huh?" He frowns. "No, I told you, the government was taxing people summat awful. Smugglers needed to feed their families; they weren't all 'wreckers'. Watch it, we're drifting."

I dig an oar deeper to turn the boat. The waves get

fiercer, as if they're guarding Cliff Point, pushing and pulling at the boat like a game of tug of war. A drizzle starts spitting at us from above too – looking up, the sky is no longer clean-paper blue, but stained and mucky with grey clouds.

"I think I see the cave entrance!" Sam bounces excitedly.

I see it too. And it's not all I see. The waves haven't finished with their stories. I picture Dad struggling to get from the boat on to the rocks as Vicious Wind batters and pummels him like a puppet; he's thrown into the water; arms flailing as the tide tugs and tears at him with other ideas for his journey; he won't escape the wave that embraces him in a tight hug, pulling him down; he can't breathe; lungs burning as they fill with water.

I should only feel despair, horror! Instead, the anger rises tsunami-like in my chest. *I am so mad at you, Dad!* Salty sea water drips down my face from nowhere. *Didn't he always tell us, the rocks were dangerous! Didn't he always have a million rules for sailing and swimming! Couldn't he have waited till morning? Till the sea was calm and him and Mum had made up?*

*Did the treasure mean that much?*

*Did the house matter more?*

*Than us?*

Sam leans towards me, rocking the boat. "Faith, you OK?" More sea water is dripping down my face.

"Why are you crying?" he says.

I rub at my face. Not sea water. For the first time since Dad never upped and left, there are tears pouring out of my eyes.

"Why did he do something so stupid, and selfish?" I hear myself shouting. I look up at Sam with a fierce glare. "I loved him. And he ruined our lives!"

"You sound like Tess Walker," Sam says sorrowfully.

I let out a deep breath that seems to have been caught in my chest for I don't know how long.

"It's too risky! It's braver not to go and find the gold coins," I say decisively, licking salt from my lips. "To face what happens next."

I thought I would drown if I cried. Instead, my head suddenly feels clearer. "Your gran does want you with her, Sam. I know she does. And if she doesn't, then you'll live with us." I nod my head firmly. "But I don't know if it'll be The Lookout. My mum might need a new home too."

"Wow, you mean it?"

I nod again. This time with a smile, a big, toothy one.

"Though you really reckon my gran will let me live with her for nowt?"

I lift the oars and push them in the opposite direction. The anger, it's subsiding, retreating like the sea at low tide. "I do!" I say loudly.

"What – so we're really friends now I'm not a ghost?"

"Yes!" I beam at him and row faster. "We were friends even when I thought you were a ghost!"

Sam's arms get jiggy again and he plonks himself up on the edge and gives me a sailor salute. "Homewards then," he says in a posh voice – just as Vicious Wind makes a sudden appearance, lazily putting out a finger and flicking him overboard.

I hear a brief cry of "I can't swim!" before he

disappears with a massive splash, too close to the rocks. I don't think or plan. I just leap. From the boat, into ice-cold water that claws at my skin; waves that don't know their own strength, still wanting to play games, tugging me this way and that. *Fight back*! I hear a voice in my head that sounds like Dad's, and I punch and push against their watery grip. Launch for Sam; grabbing the neck of his life jacket.

"Kick your legs!" I order him as I flop on to my back, kicking my own fiercely, dragging him along with me. I've only ever life-saved with a giggly Asha in the town swimming pool and I'm sure I'm not doing it right; chilled, salty water shoots up my nose and plugs my throat; my shoulders and arms ache from keeping Sam's head above the water.

It seems an age, though it probably only takes a few minutes, before the sea finally spits us out, as if we don't taste so good after all. Just in time – the dirty blue sky is now a charcoal grey, and hailstones appear from nowhere, spiky and hard, as we crawl and splutter our way out of the shallows, back to where we left our stuff. Sam retches up sea water, his (clean for once) face a funny shade of green. Then: "You saved my life," he whispers. I'm still taking it all in. I pass him a towel while he *finally* takes off his parka. Wrapped up, we crouch down beneath the rock overhang in silent shock and watch the yellow-and-blue dinghy blowing around, smashing against the rocks, till it blasts off into the distance.

"Let's face it, we don't even know the gold coins are definitely there." I eventually speak between chattering teeth. "All Tess Walker said in her letter was she'd hide the '*treasure in time*'."

"Treasure in time," Sam repeats.

"*Treasure in time*." The last word pings around every corner of my brain like a pinball machine. "There was a small key in the tin box!" I picture the initials scratched into the door of our clock. "T.W.!" I shout louder, as the hail storms the rocks above us. "*Tess Walker! Not Tom!*"

"You what?" Sam gives me a sideways look like I've drunk too much sea water.

"I think I know where the treasure is!" I reach forward and clasp both of Sam's hands without thinking. Not in the yucky way that Asha likes to daydream about holding hands with her latest crush. In an I'm-glad-we're-in-this-together way.

"The cross carved on our many-greats-grandfather clock! I think Tess hid the treasure there and marked the spot!"

"That's why it's so heavy?" Sam joins in, squeezing my hands.

"Tom Walker must have found it after Tess died. He stopped time, locking and gluing the door shut." Keeping his secrets in, along with the treasure. I'm halfway trying to explain this to Sam as another different sound erupts above us. A roaring, rumbling noise that's not like thunder or a sea storm. It's the sound of a ship lurching or an angry giant waking from centuries of sleep. Rocks tumble down on to the beach in the near distance. The cliff beneath The Lookout – it's falling.

# Twenty

If a giant *has* woken up, then he's reached down with a knife and taken a cake slice out of the cliff. I rub water from my eyes as the hail keeps falling. The end of my garden has sheared away. That's our greenhouse half-dangling from the edge! Only the metal frame; the glass panes have shattered on the rocks below. I shudder with urgent fear, until I picture Noah, safe at Exeter hospital with Mum.

"Look!" Sam shouts beside me. I stare further up. I wasn't imagining it before

– my tower room *is* leaning, like a bent wizard's hat. We look at each other and instinctively start to run. Crossing the sodden shingle as quickly as it'll let us, up the stairs, along the cliff, the towels round our shoulders billowing like capes.

Closer to the house, I can see thick black lines scarring The Lookout's pebbledash cream walls.

"It's collapsing," Sam says, clutching at my arm to stop me getting closer. I let him; there's nothing I can do now – until I see a familiar dark head passing beyond The Lookout's fence.

"Uncle Art!" I bolt away from Sam's grasp.

Hail hits my face as I chase my uncle to the back of the house. I catch a painful breath as I see it: The Crack is almost at the cliff edge, longer, wider, and separating our garden in two.

"Uncle Art, no!" He's at the back door. He's smashed a window; now he's reaching in to unlock it. "It's not safe!"

"Faith, don't!" Sam's voice joins mine as he rounds the corner.

Uncle Art glances back, his face both scared

and severe. "Is it your doing? This Mr Cow-askey interfering with my council visit? Just tell me where this treasure is!" he shouts, his voice desperate.

I think about just telling him, but by the time Uncle Art has the clock open, the house might have buried him! As if The Lookout's reading my thoughts, an almighty creaking noise cuts through the air, like the house is shrieking with pain.

"Uncle Art, come back!" I plead with him, my eyes blurring from a mix of hail and tears.

"We have to go!" Sam is pulling at me again, pointing frantically at the end of the garden – it's moving, slipping off the edge like a waterfall of soil. "It'll take us with it!"

A rumble, then a flash of lightening above, like a crack in the sky.

"Uncle Art!" I shout again as his sodden back retreats inside.

I don't know how to stop him! I hear Mrs Hollowbread, what she said about the parents looking more anxious than their children.

"It's not fair!" I scream through more rumbling

above. "Uncle Art, it's not *fair* that Grandpa made Dad guardian of The Lookout when you're the eldest! It's not fair Dad kept secrets from you!"

I catch my breath.

"The Lookout's not worth dying for, Uncle Art! It's just slate and stone. Think about Aunty Val!"

I let out a watery exhale of relief as Uncle Art's head appears back in the doorway. I can't tell by his expression if he's angry or anguished, but I have his attention.

"I just *want*—" he starts to say, right as the left wall of the house makes a hideous whining noise, before it bends and collapses like a knee joint. Uncle Art jumps back, bounding into us, as slate tiles start falling off my tower roof like knives.

We are running, all three of us, slipping on grass that's been turned to mud by hail and rain, away from the edge; off the cliff path; back to the sturdy brick pillbox that's been Sam's home for weeks.

We stare out from the dry safety of its doorway, and we can only watch through a curtain of ice and water – Uncle Art, me and Sam – as one side of The

Lookout seems to implode into itself. Another wedge of garden gets sliced away. Until my broken house gets so close to the edge it's almost stepping off the cliff.

# Twenty-one

*Four months later.*

We're standing in a line, me, Mum, Noah. A strong wind that seems less mean, more mischievous, zips in and out, getting busy with hair and cheeky with skirts. The town mayor finishes speaking as Cheeky Wind lifts her dress; she holds it down, quickly cuts the ribbon, and the cloth drops away to reveal the new plaque. There's some clapping and one "hooray" (DS Strangler) and a finger-whistle (Mr Kowalski).

It was Mr Kowalski who arranged it. "The past does not always need to be honourable to be historical. Look at Henry the Eighth!"

That's why our house is now protected by The Preservation Society. What's left of it that is, a skeleton of stone and wood and fireplaces, with no doors and few walls. Nature's already claiming the rooms as its own: grass and foliage and bird nests have replaced our belongings, which loads of people from town helped us to recover the day after the storm.

"Now I want you all to point, big smiles." The photographer from our local paper starts arranging me and Mum and Noah in front of the plaque, below the hot summer sky. "How about a thumbs-up!"

"Bit cheesy?" Mum says under her breath and keeps her arms folded. Noah doesn't even hear the request, he's away with his fairies, no doubt thinking of the beachcombing he and Sam will do soon as this is finished.

I push forward both thumbs; huge smile. I don't mind cheesy any more. I'm proud as punch of the plaque. The photographer clicks. Mum relents and makes a mild thumbs-up with a nudge in my side, "Oi, you," when I giggle. We're a safe distance from the edge, on the new diverted coastal path; there's a gate around The Lookout and a warning sign to stop anyone going inside. Not because there's anything left to steal; most of the slate from the roof shattered on to the beach or got pilfered. (Aunty Val wouldn't let Uncle Art take anything. She reckons the house is cursed.) No, the gate and sign are there because the rest of the house might fall off the edge any moment. No one knows when. But it will happen. One day.

"Pretend like you're reading it!" The photographer instructs us. Mum and I (Noah's busy with his fairies) adopt pensive eyes, like we're ramblers who've just stumbled across the plaque, dated from March:

"...*a storm broke off part of the cliff, removing The Lookout's back garden... Beneath the house is evidence of smugglers' tunnels from late 1700s...*"

Ramblers will read and make furtive glances at what's left of my tower room, where Tom Walker would, *usually*, light his lantern to warn ships. They'll peer at the broken pebbledash walls standing shard-like, as they learn more about the smugglers' tunnels beneath. Stand on tiptoes to get a glance of the hallway, where the grandfather clock with its treasure was still standing after the worst of the landslip was over. And they might get a funny feeling in their stomachs, at the thought that lives can fall, just like that, slide right over the edge.

"Make sure you write about the town museum," Sam's telling the photographer, eyes determined and as blue as his new summer jacket, stabbing a finger at the QR code on the plaque. Sam's worked hard on the town museum's new website. After Mrs Hollowbread's house, the museum's still like his second home. Except he hasn't got it to himself now. The museum has had to dust down its elderly volunteers (as well as its floors and walls), because it seems that everyone wants to visit the new exhibition: "The Story of The Lookout". To see Tess Walker's letter and her miniature portrait. To read about the wrecking of the *Providence* and how Tess bravely tried to save the sailors. And of course, to see the gold coin the museum's been allowed to keep.

It was hard to say who the gold belonged to when we finally opened up our many-greats-grandfather clock and found a treasure chest inside. Well, except *Providence*. (Or, if you're Uncle Art: "It's mine!") Mum agreed with me that The Preservation Society should take charge of it and the chest of gold eventually got sold to The British Museum for safekeeping. The Preservation Society split the profit between the museum (now it preserves memories with interactive buttons) – and us. So we could find a new house (that's slowly becoming a home).

It's a hard business, this memory preserving. Mr Kowalski has created a tourist trail about the smugglers' tunnels that has more people supping at The Ship Inn and visiting St Swithun's than ever before. It takes them past Halfpenny Farm and the disused well and on to the pillbox – which apparently used to be The Lookout's pig pen! Sam found out its blocked-up tunnel was secretly dug out again in the

Second World War (The Lookout's good at keeping secrets). And then, finally, the trail reaches The Lookout and Cliff Point.

Noah's now got a new gig in show-and-tell – he's become a small celebrity at school. Even scaredy-cat Edie Miller likes to hear his ghost stories. Because Noah still reckons there *are* other ghosts. Even though I tell him ghosts only exist when their stories get told.

Then there's Sam, always making us fundraise for the town museum, because he still worries "you never get owt for nowt", even though Mrs Hollowbread spoils him something rotten (*err, new trainers, Sam?*).

Sian has proved a whizz at getting money. Though she and Sam constantly come to blows about how to spend it at our weekly candyfloss milkshake meeting. Asha and I, we roll our eyes and wait till it passes and they're friends again and we can take a selfie – #matesmakinhistory so everyone keeps visiting the museum and hearing the story of The Lookout.

I won't lie (well, I did promise Dad not to): The Crack might not have split me in two in the end, but there's a fracture deep inside me, like a shadowy line on an X-ray, that I worry will never heal, not properly. But I can ignore it mostly, if I keep Dad alive in my head. My own personal ghost. Like right now, he's standing next to me, Mischievous Wind playing with his red-grey hair, lines framing his smiling eyes, as we stare across together at our old house at the very, *very* edge of the cliff.

It's easy to imagine him placing his large hand around mine, a finger-squeeze, as we agree: that you can never really know when things might fall, but, as long as there are others to keep you back from the edge, you'll be all right.

# Acknowledgements

This is a story about loss and finding a home, so I'm very lucky that my book has found its own amazing home with some very fine folk indeed.

A huge thank you to Kate Shaw, super-agent, who goes beyond the call of duty in reading, advising and championing; wise as well as witty. To all at the wonderful house of Nosy Crow – you have my heartfelt gratitude – what a fantastic publishing family to belong to. Extra thanks to the very brilliant Kirsty Stansfield, for helping make Faith's story so much better – I couldn't ask for a lovelier, more talented editor to work alongside. And, also, to the amazing, eagle-eyed Lauren Fairgrieve. Plus, a bright felt-tipped thank you to the gifted design team and Kathrin Honesta for the stunning cover – those waves!

Thank you to the larger net that holds my storyteller life: my local library and bookshops, my book club and writer pals (thanks to Fleur especially). Thank you to those who read earlier drafts, for your encouraging words, both the younger: Mae, Sophie, Tilda, Sammy, and the older: Lucy, Joy, Nicky, Toni (aka my mum).

Closer still to home – thank you to the three brave hearts who sail with me making memories: Duncs, Chief Tea Maker (and so much more!). Laurie, for continuing to crack me up with your impressions and jokes, even when I'm nagging you about homework. Mae, for sparking the idea that became this story, and inspiring me with your unique spirit, both afraid and fearless.

Finally, thank you, Reader, for stepping inside my story and welcoming Faith and Noah and Sam into your heads and homes.

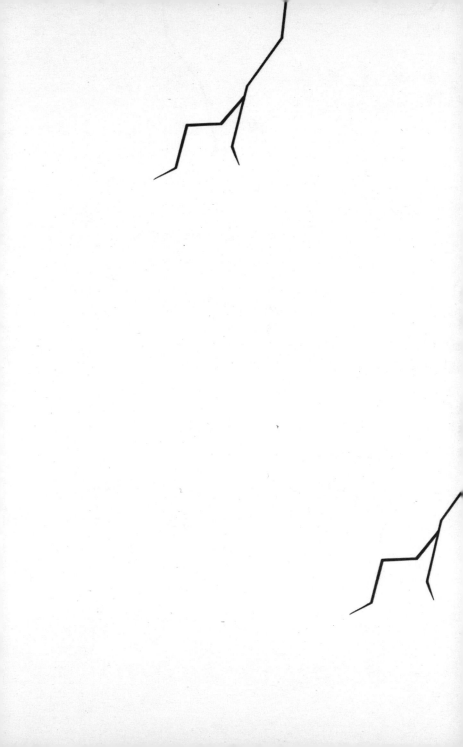

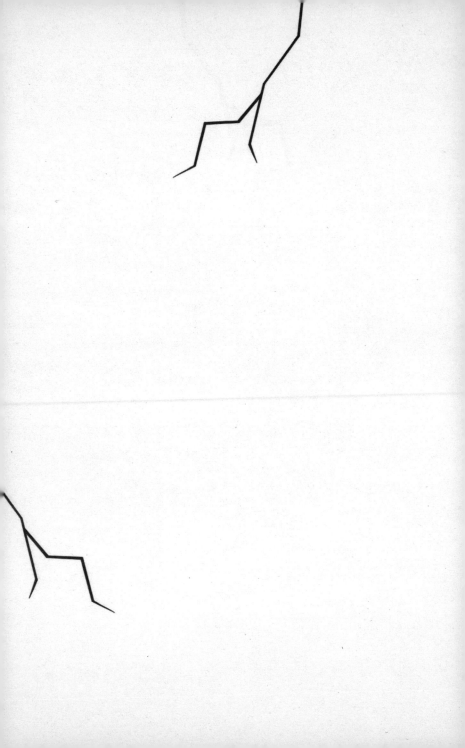

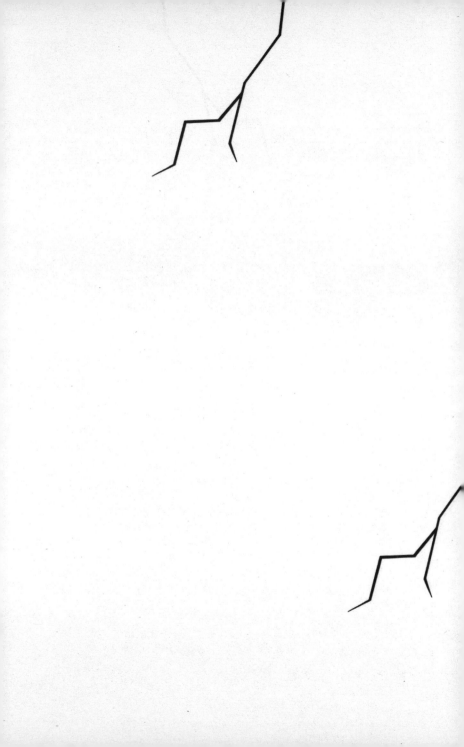

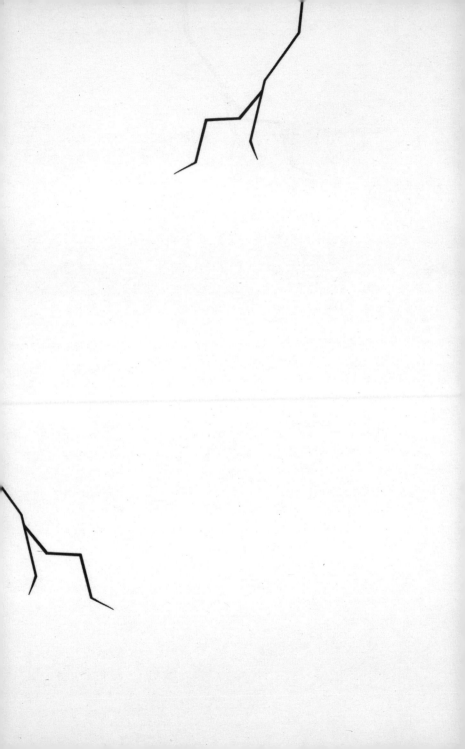

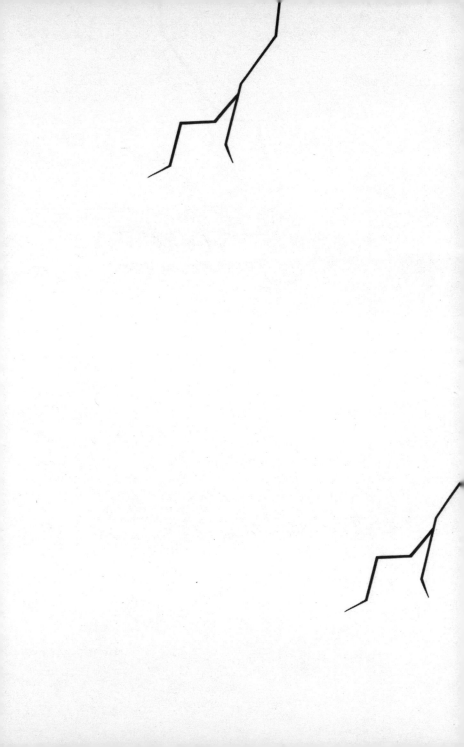

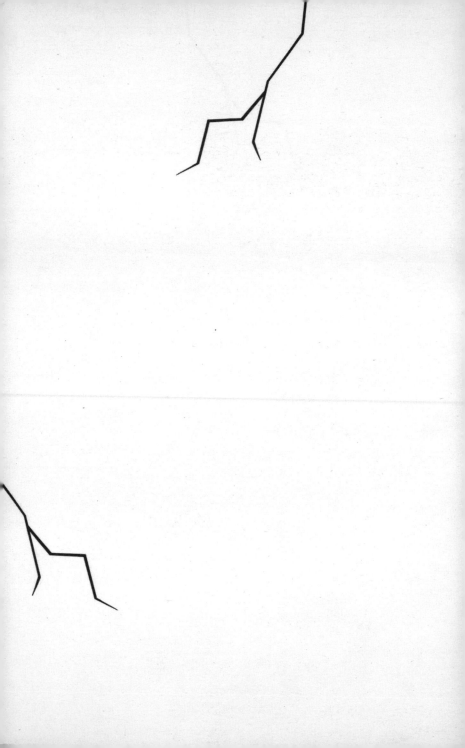